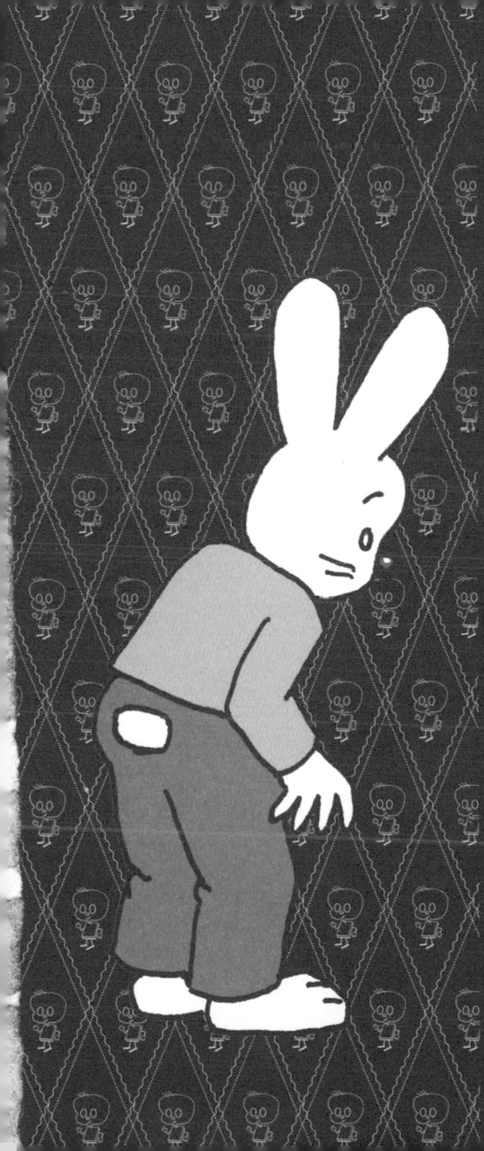

JACK AND THE BOX

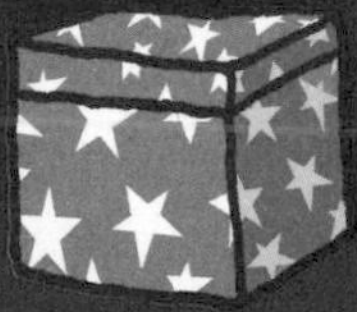

art spiegelman

JACK AND THE BOX

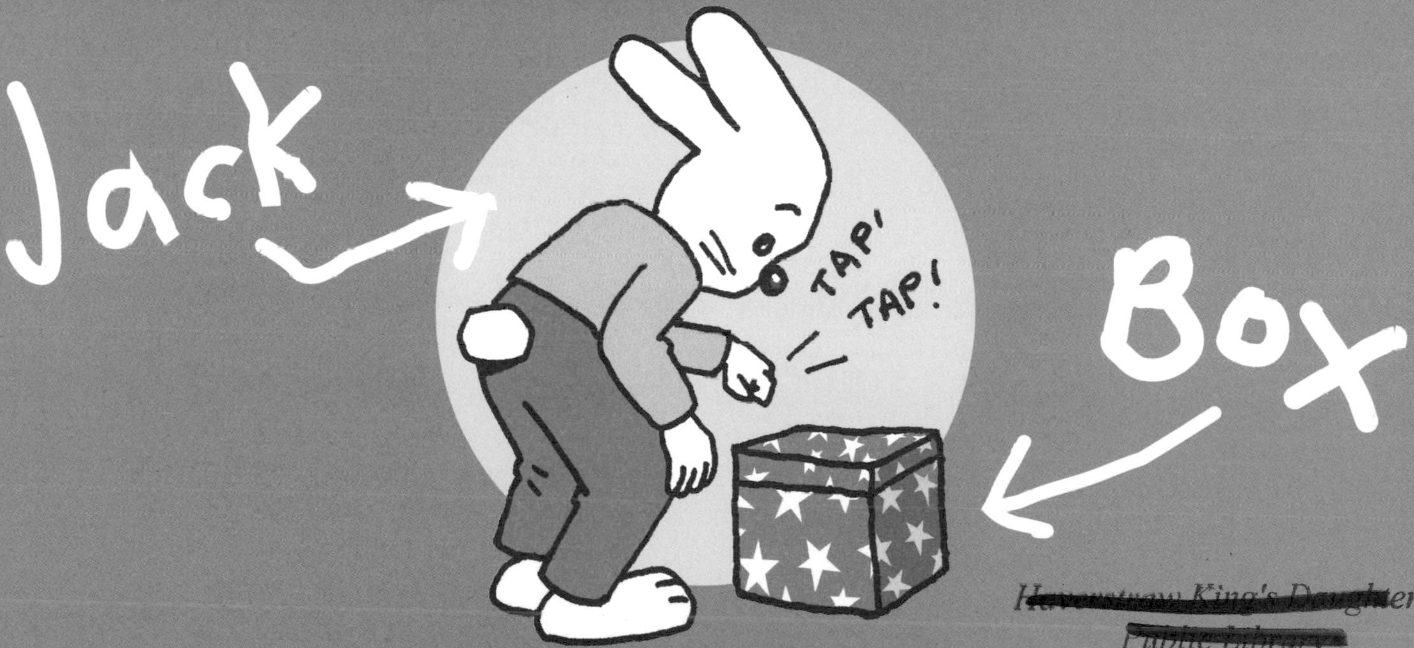
Jack
TAP! TAP!
Box

A TOON BOOK BY

art spiegelman

THE LITTLE LIT LIBRARY, A DIVISION OF RAW JUNIOR, LLC, NEW YORK

Editorial Director: FRANÇOISE MOULY
Advisor: ART SPIEGELMAN

Book Design: FRANÇOISE MOULY, JONATHAN BENNETT & ART SPIEGELMAN

Library of Congress Control Number: 2007910340
ISBN 13: 978-0-9799238-3-8 ISBN 10: 0-9799238-3-8

10 9 8 7 6 5 4 3 2 1

www.TOON-BOOKS.com

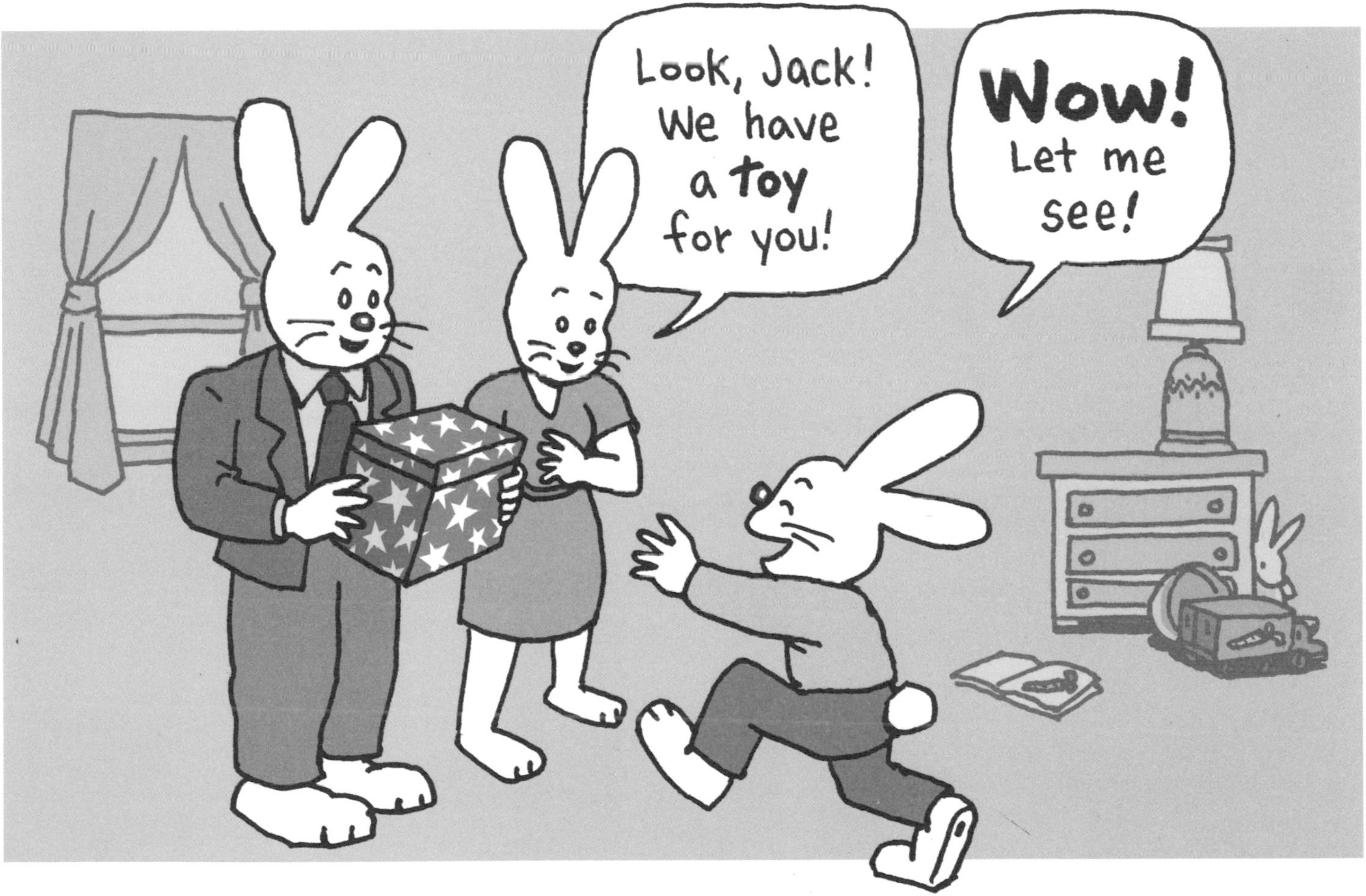
Look, Jack! We have a **toy** for you!
Wow! Let me see!

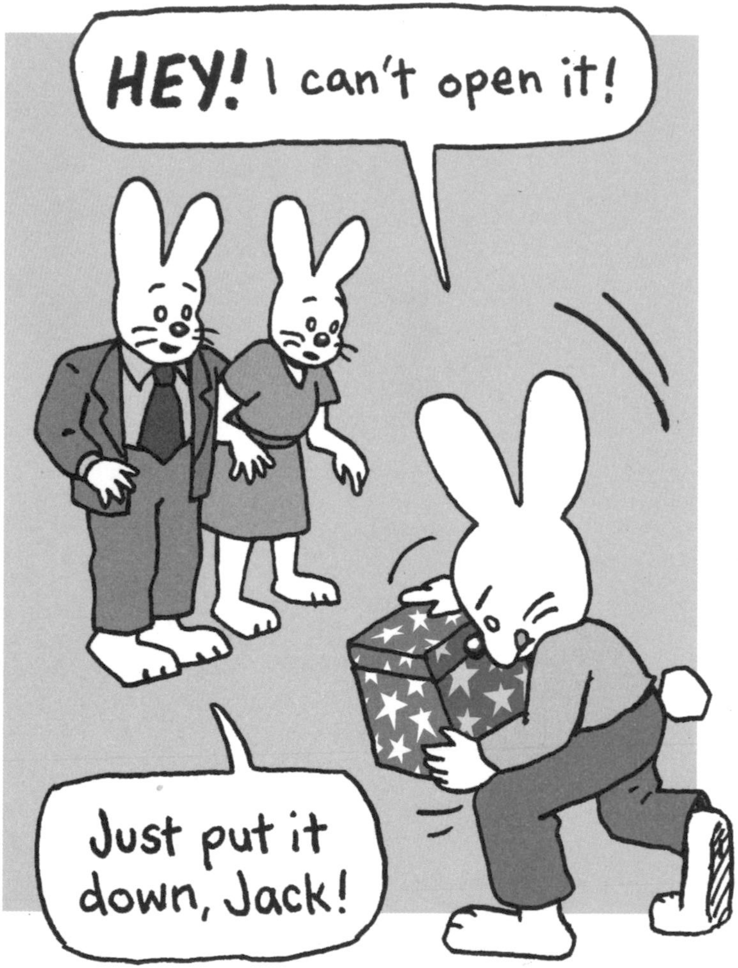
HEY! I can't open it!
Just put it down, Jack!

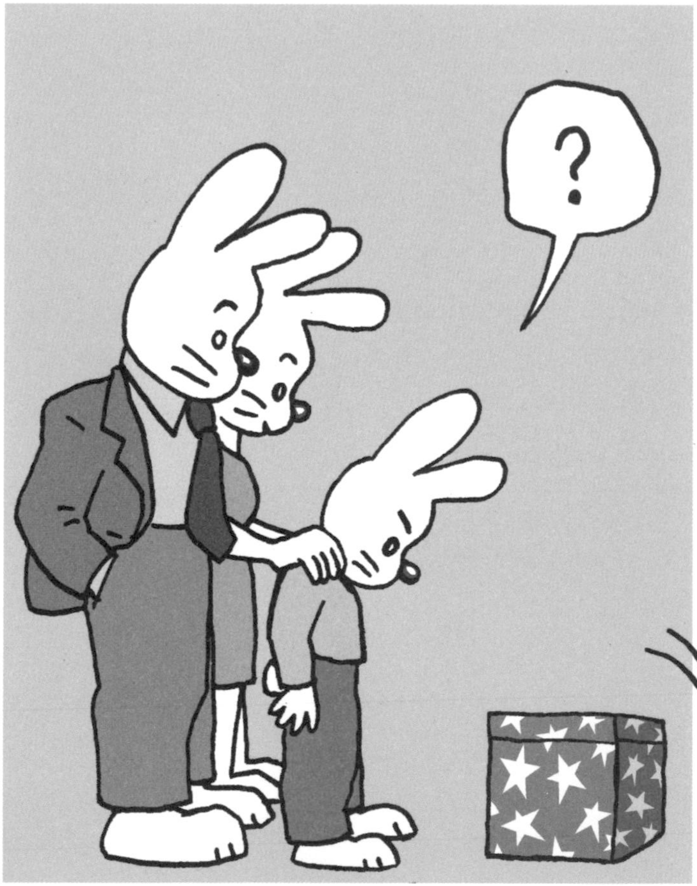
?

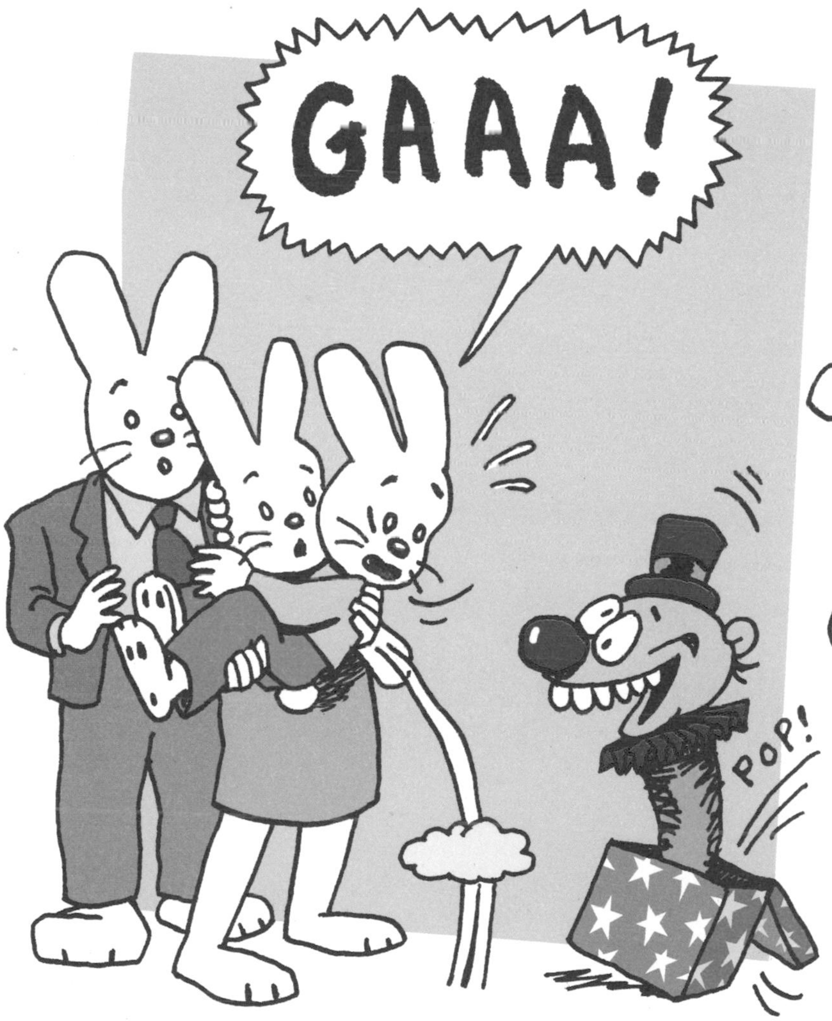
GAAA!
POP!

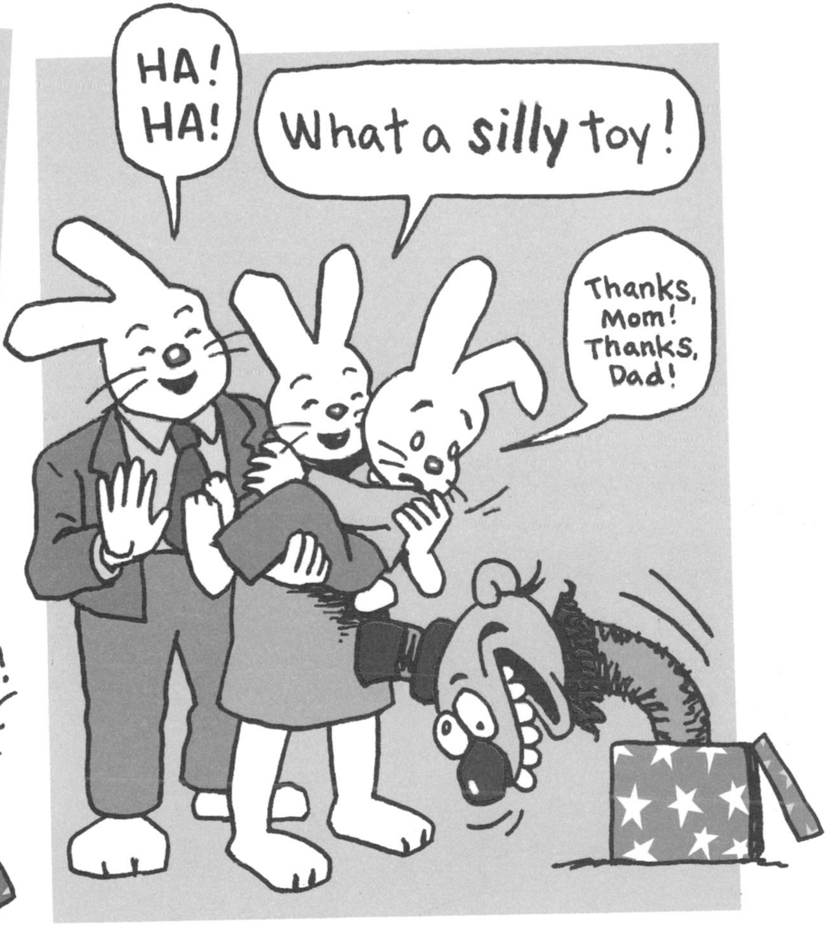
HA! HA!
What a silly toy!
Thanks, Mom! Thanks, Dad!

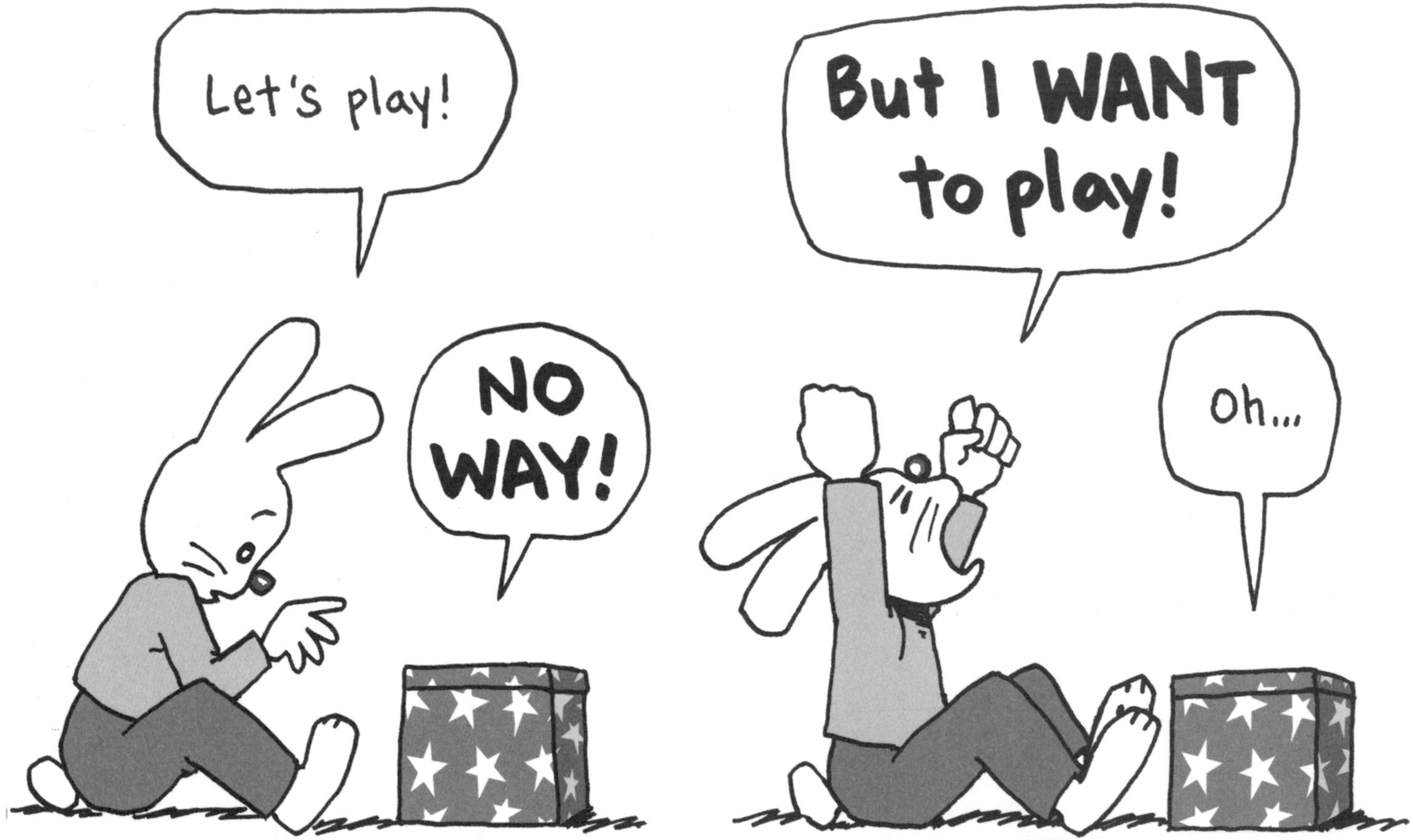
Let's play!
NO WAY!
But I WANT to play!
Oh...

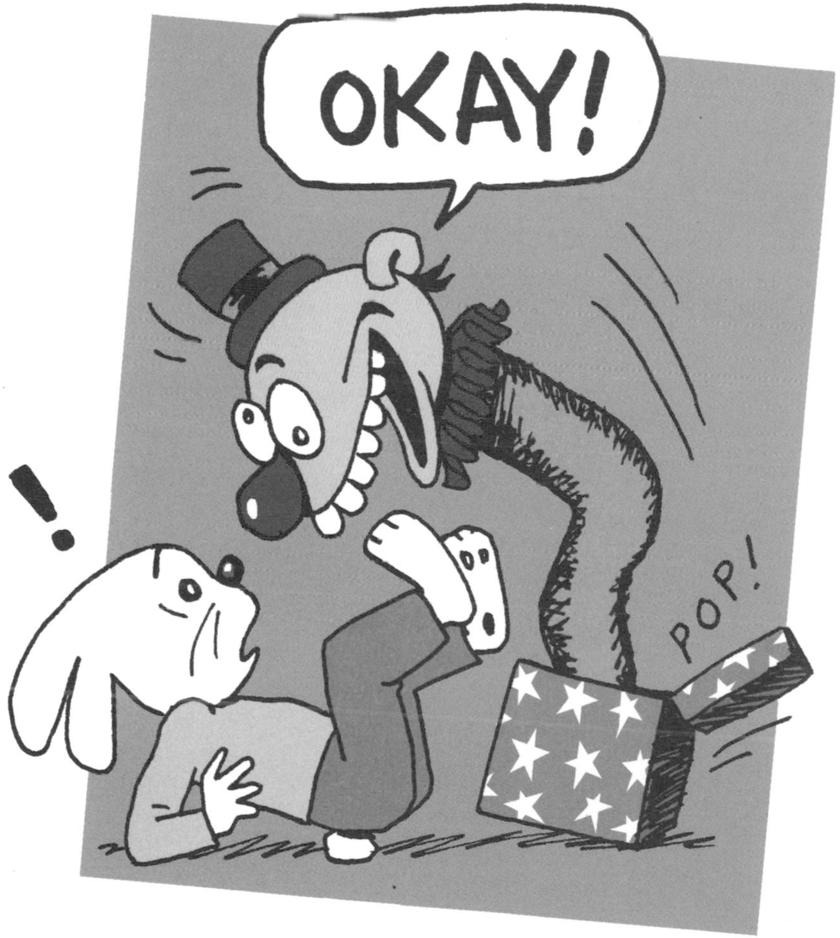
OKAY!
!
POP!

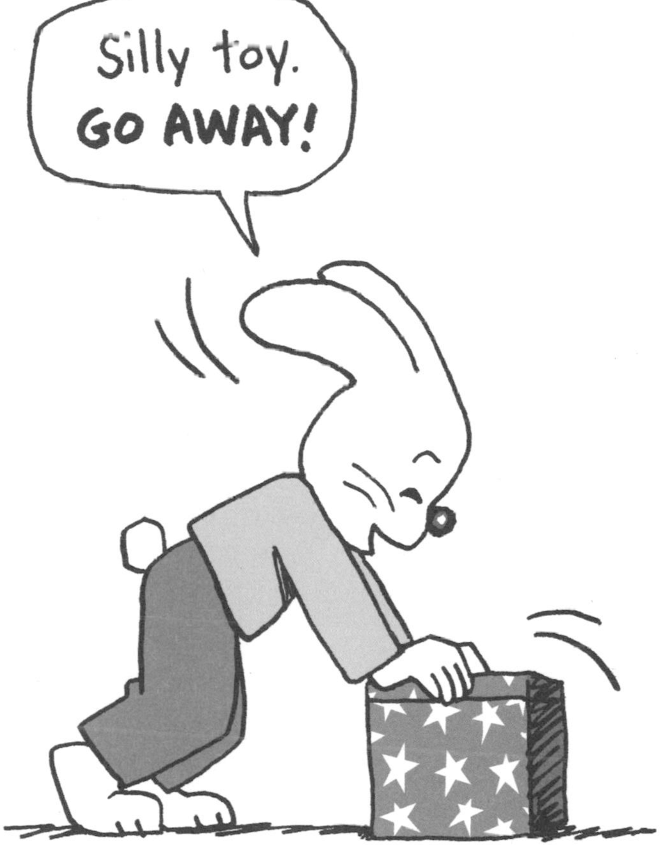
Silly toy.
GO AWAY!

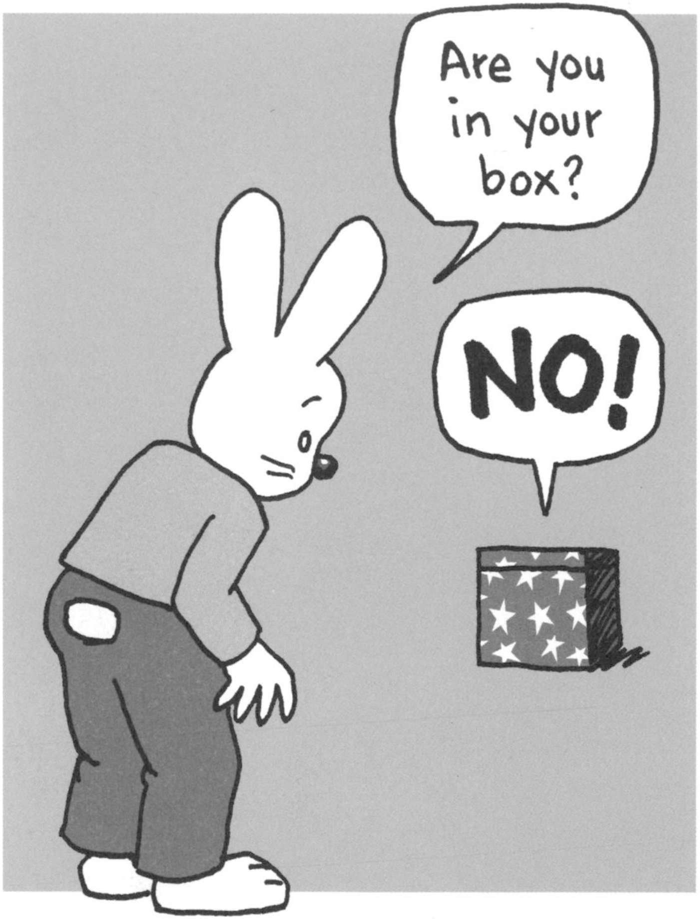
Are you in your box?
NO!

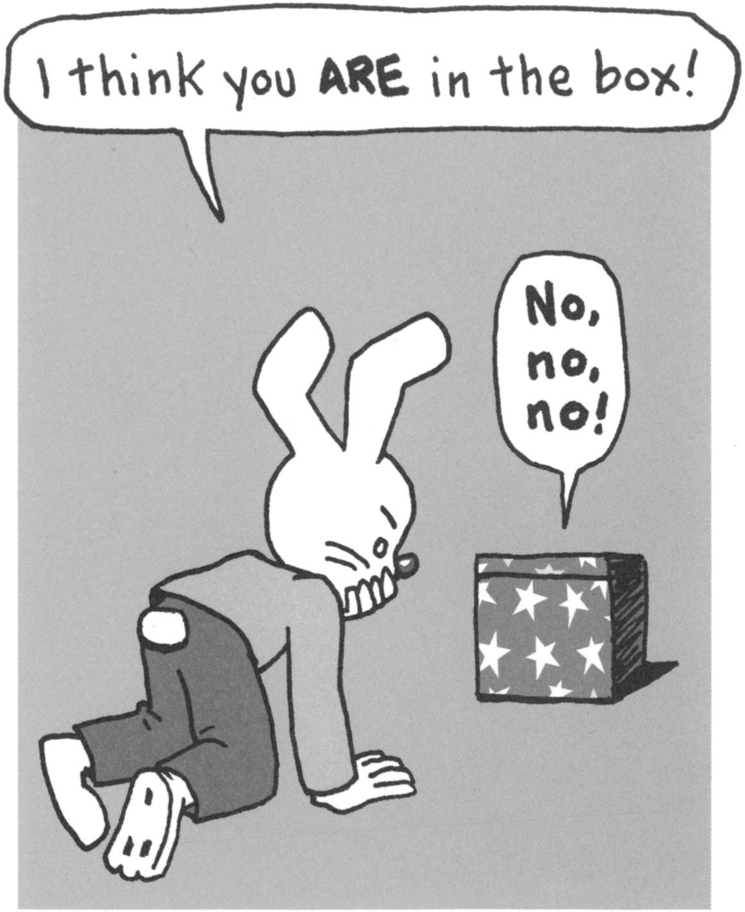
I think you **ARE** in the box!
No, no, no!

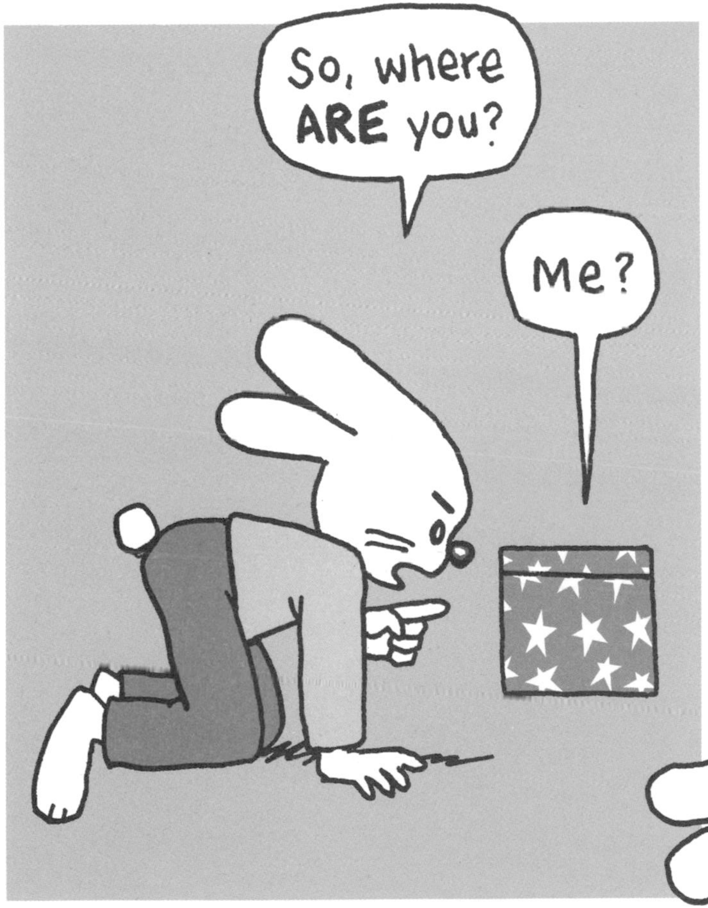
So, where ARE you?
Me?

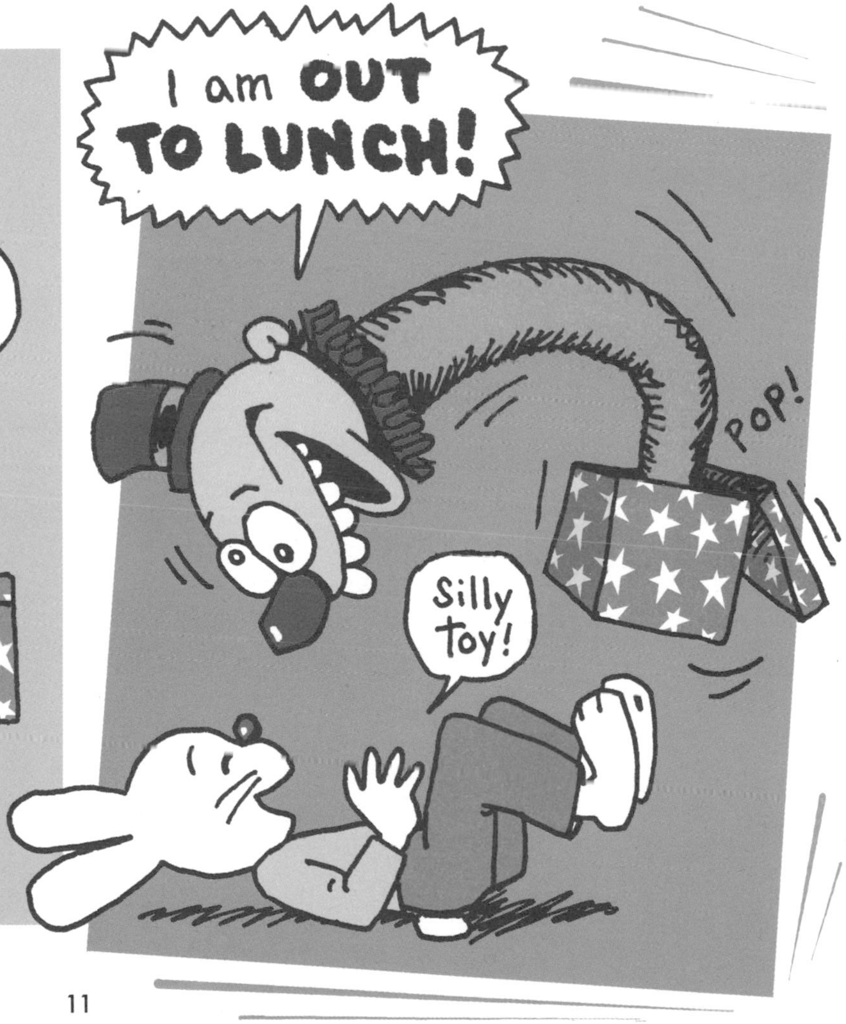
I am OUT TO LUNCH!
POP!
Silly toy!

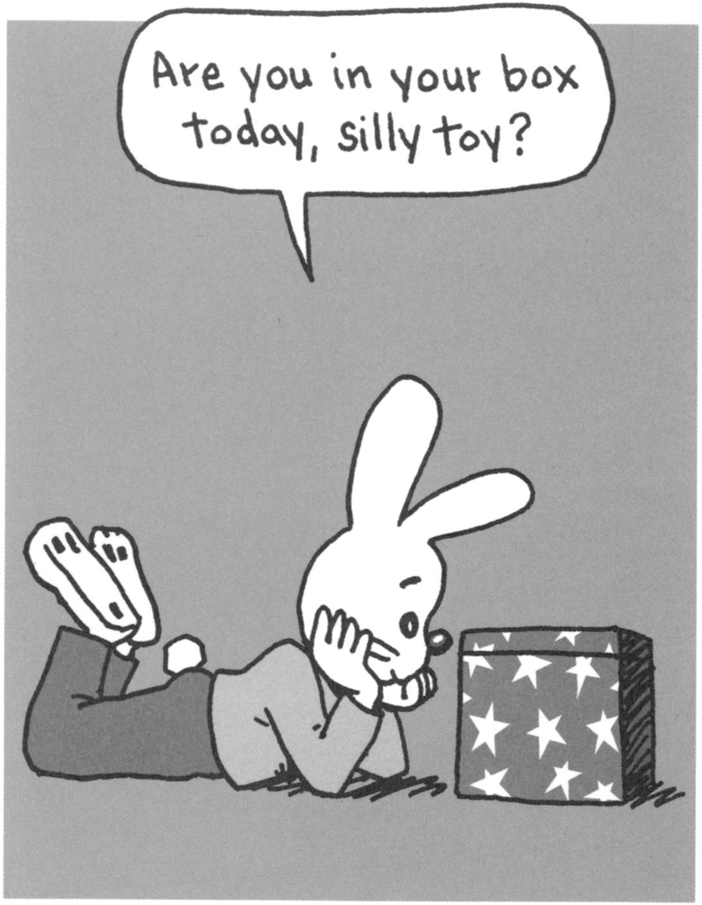
Are you in your box today, silly toy?

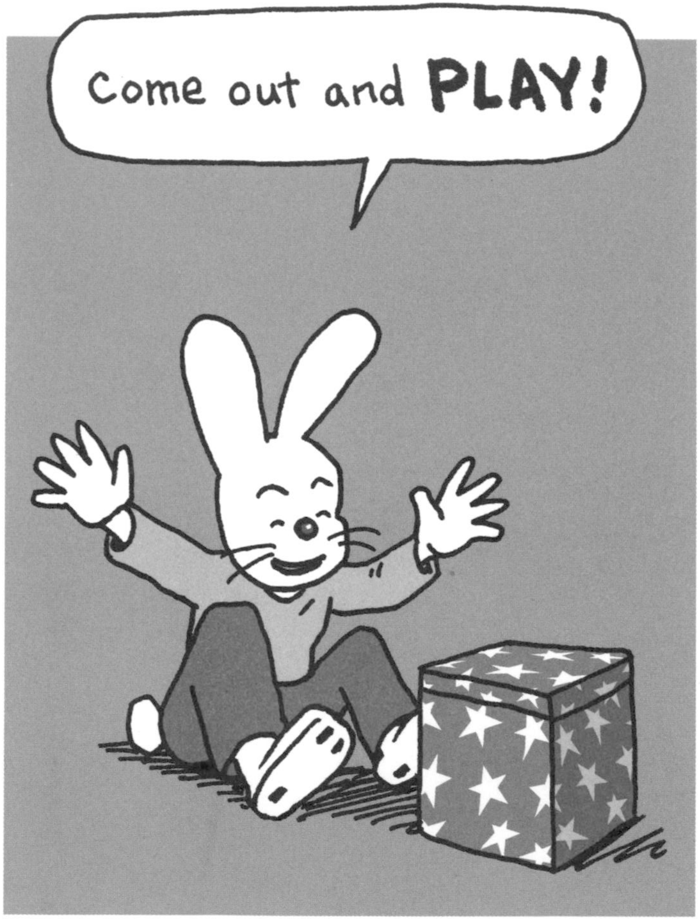
Come out and PLAY!

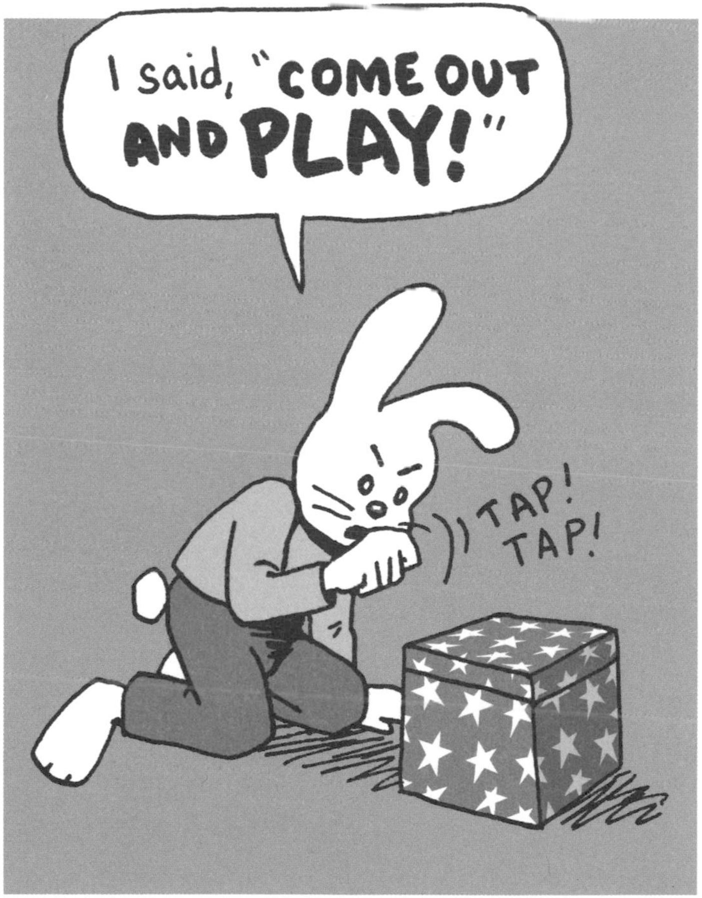
I said, "COME OUT AND PLAY!"
TAP! TAP!

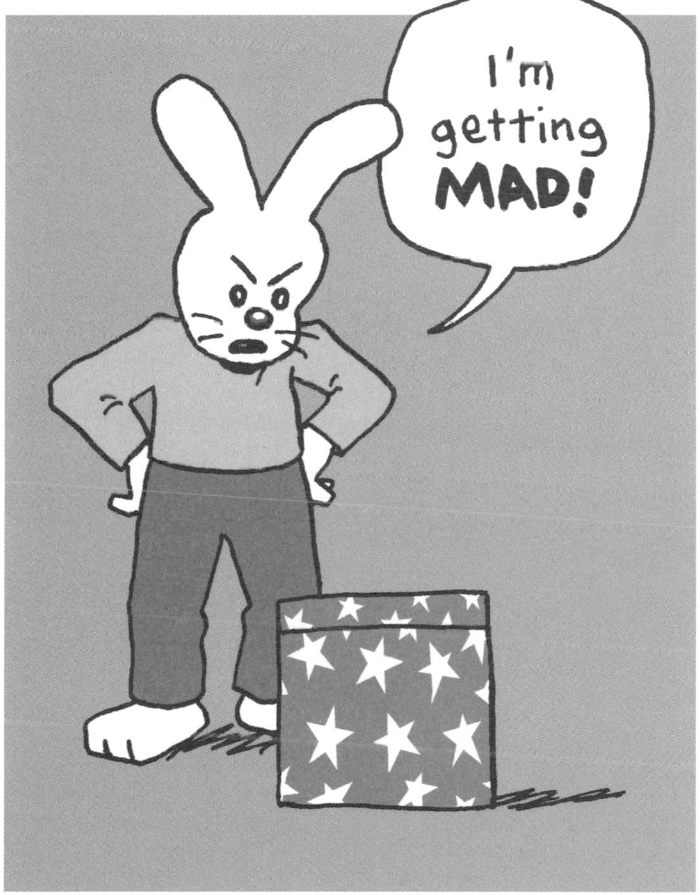
I'm getting MAD!

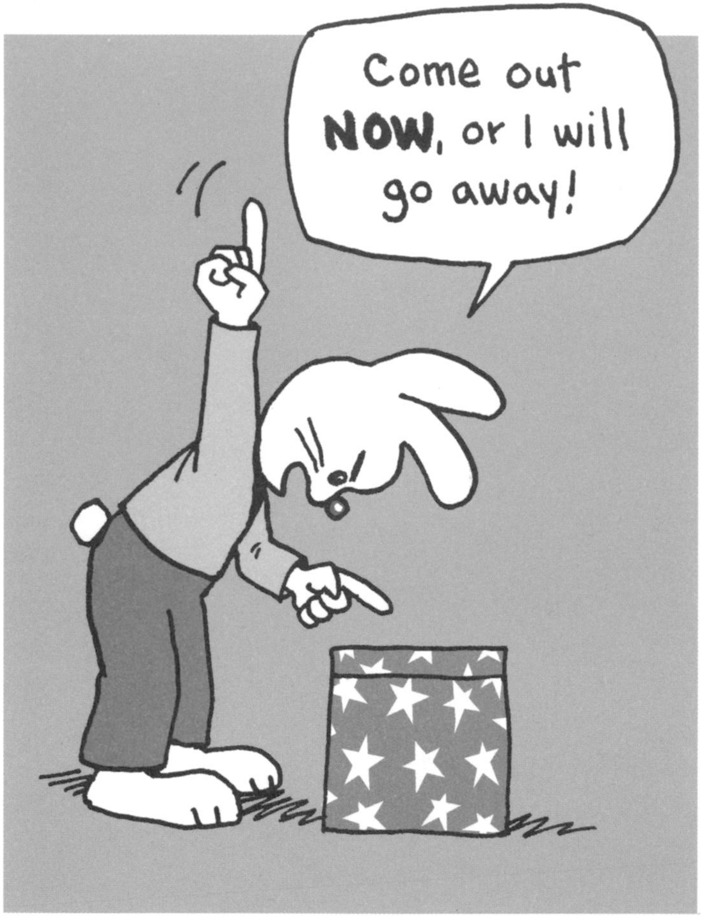
Come out NOW, or I will go away!

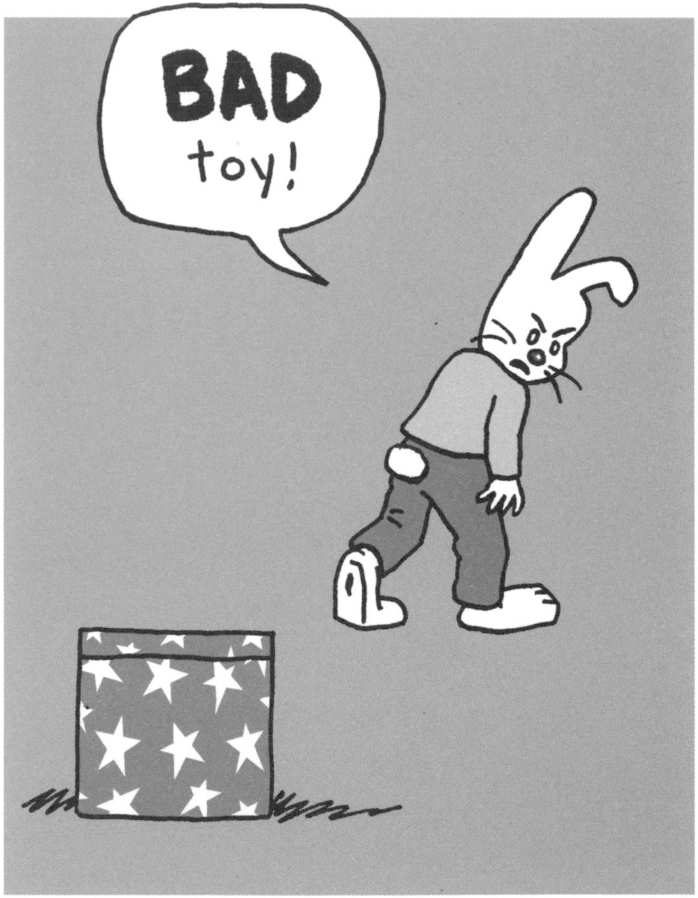
BAD toy!

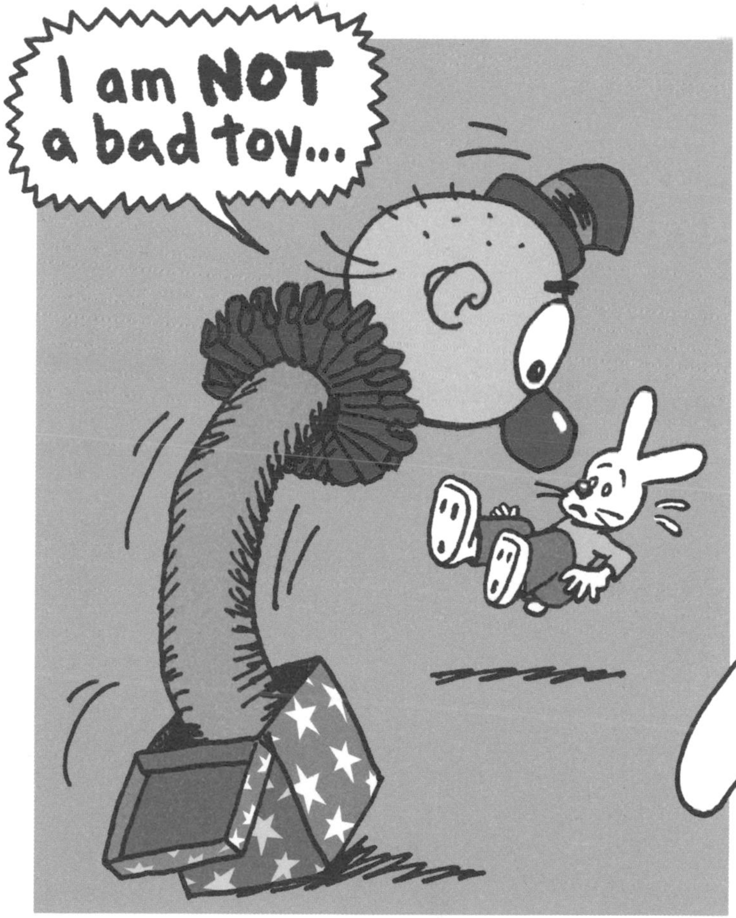
I am NOT a bad toy...

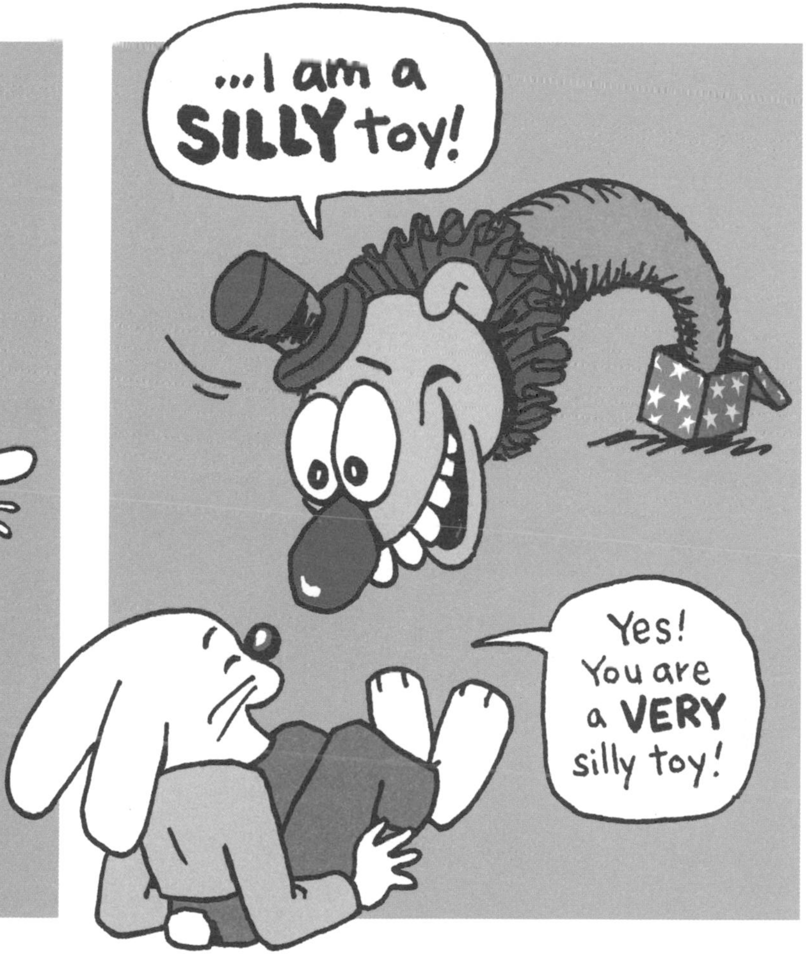
...I am a SILLY toy!
Yes! You are a VERY silly toy!

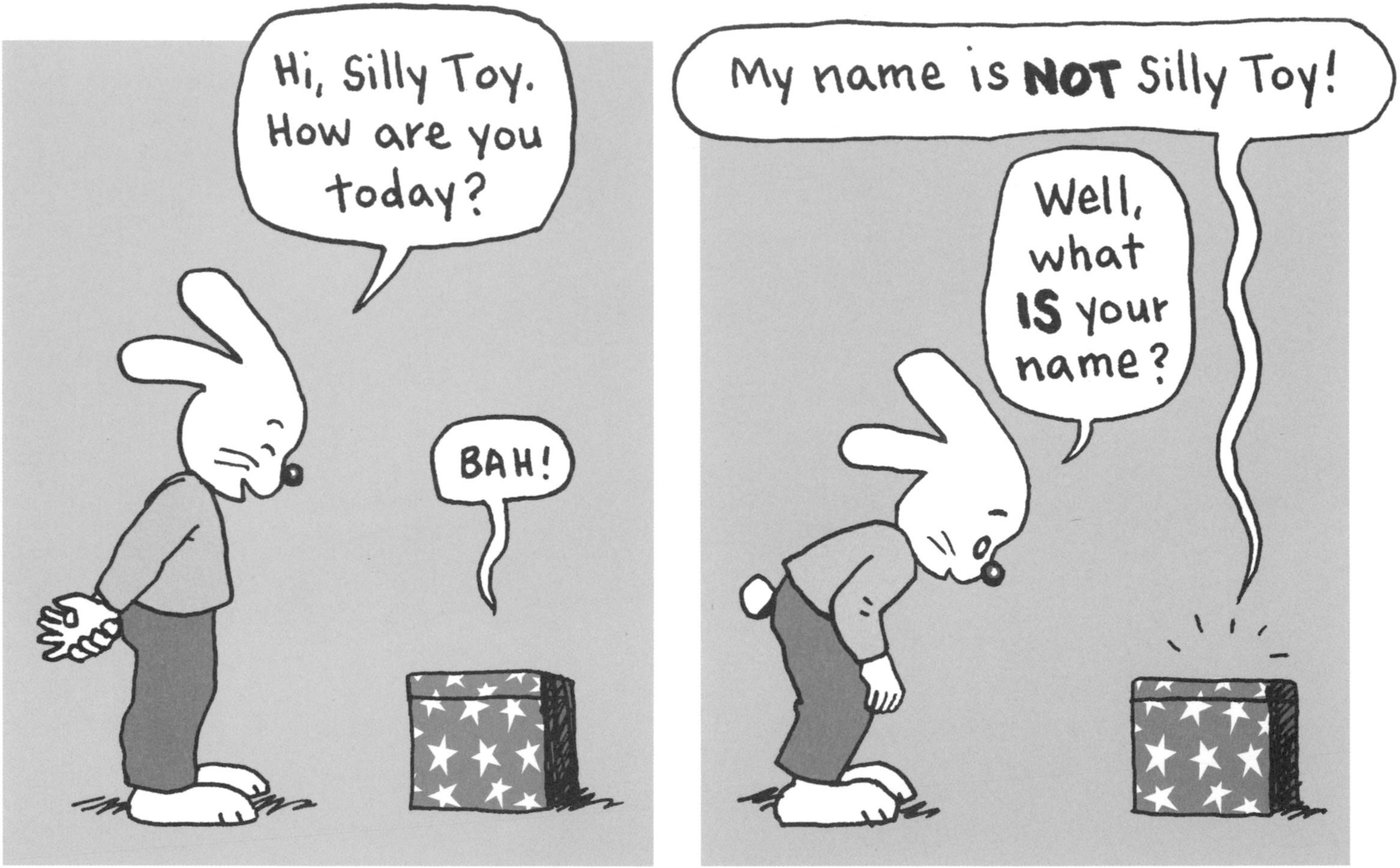
Hi, Silly Toy. How are you today?
BAH!
My name is **NOT** Silly Toy!
Well, what **IS** your name?

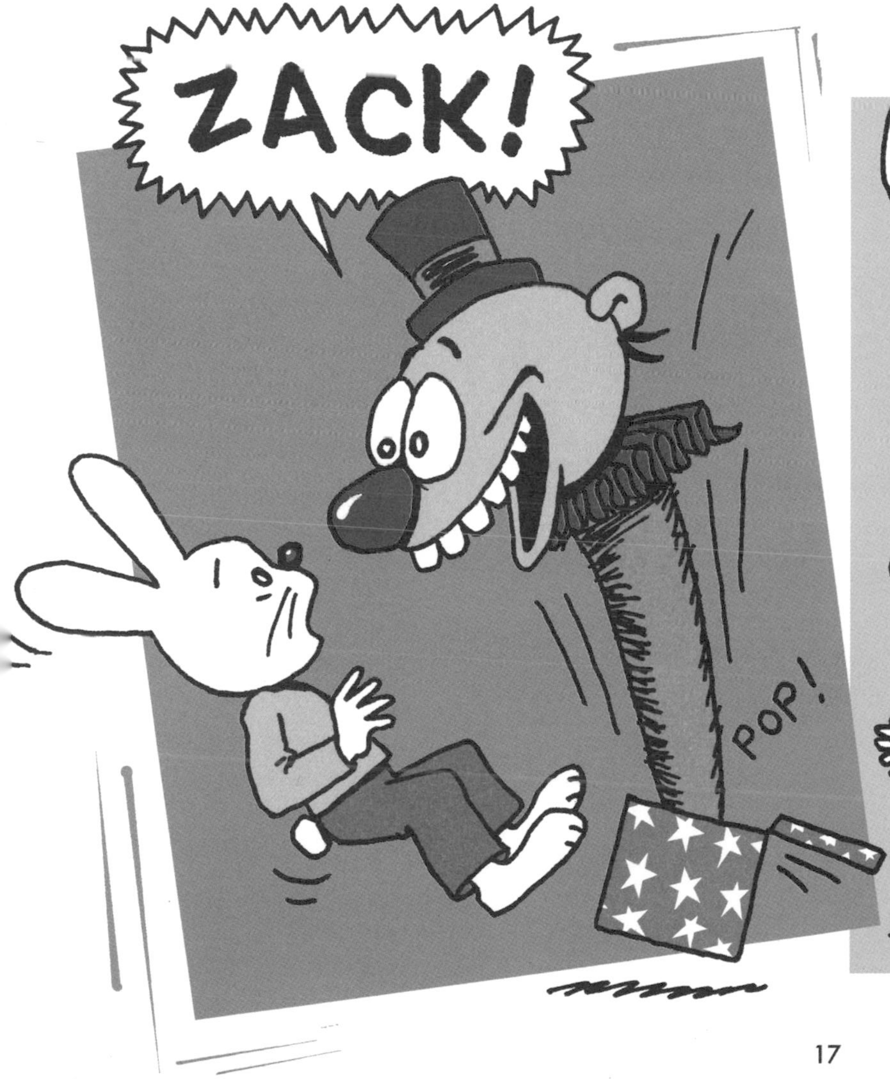
ZACK!
POP!

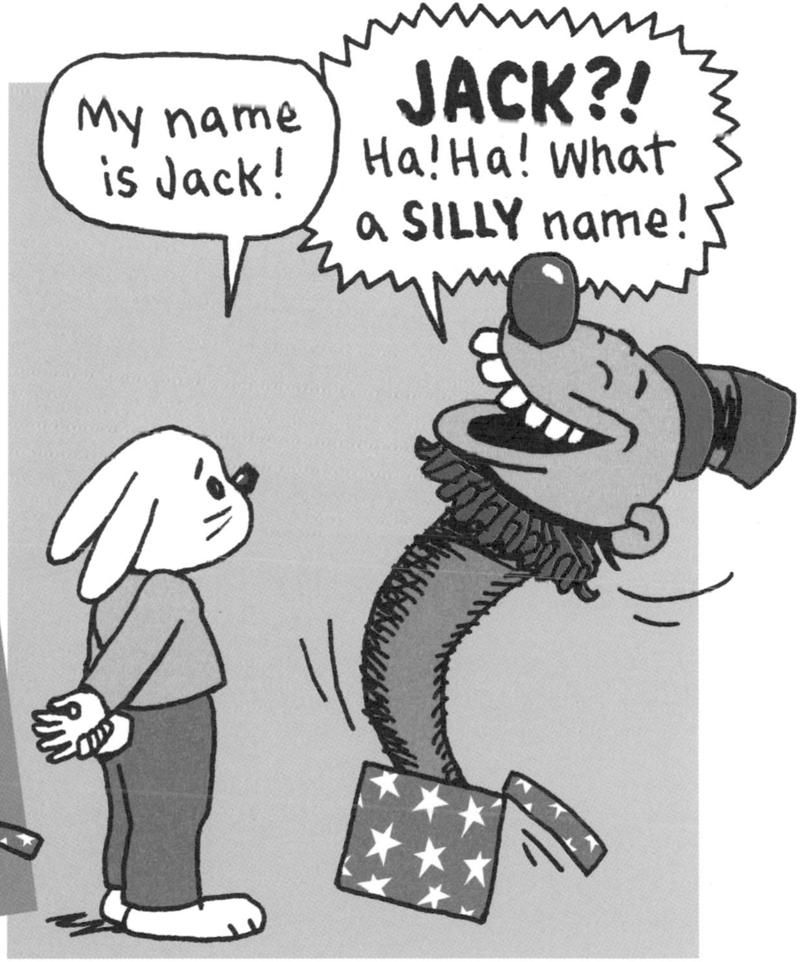
My name is Jack!
JACK?! Ha! Ha! What a SILLY name!

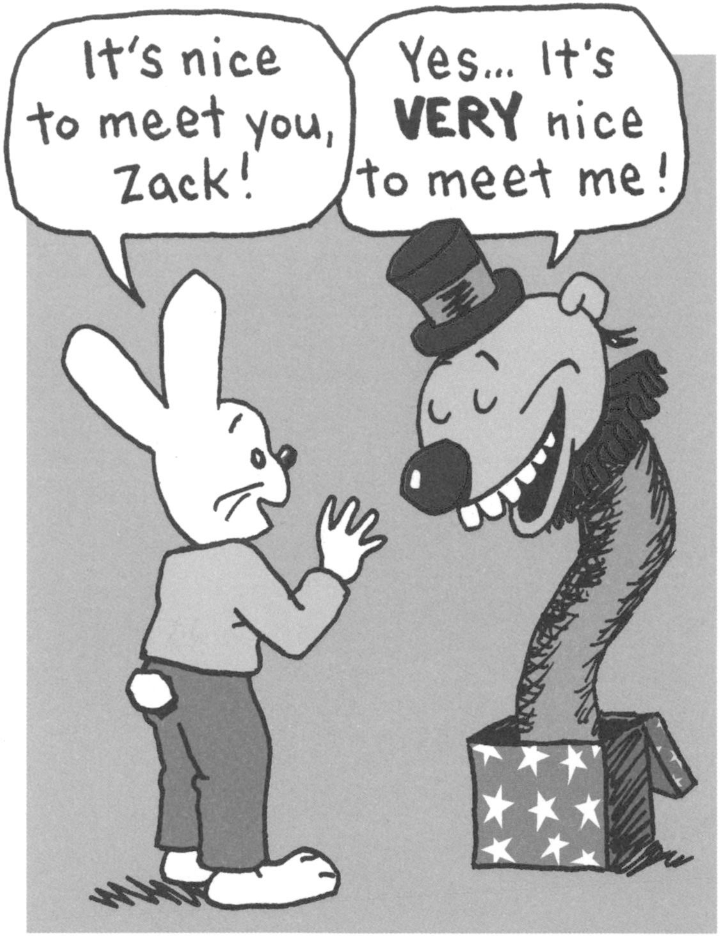
It's nice to meet you, Zack!
Yes... It's **VERY** nice to meet me!

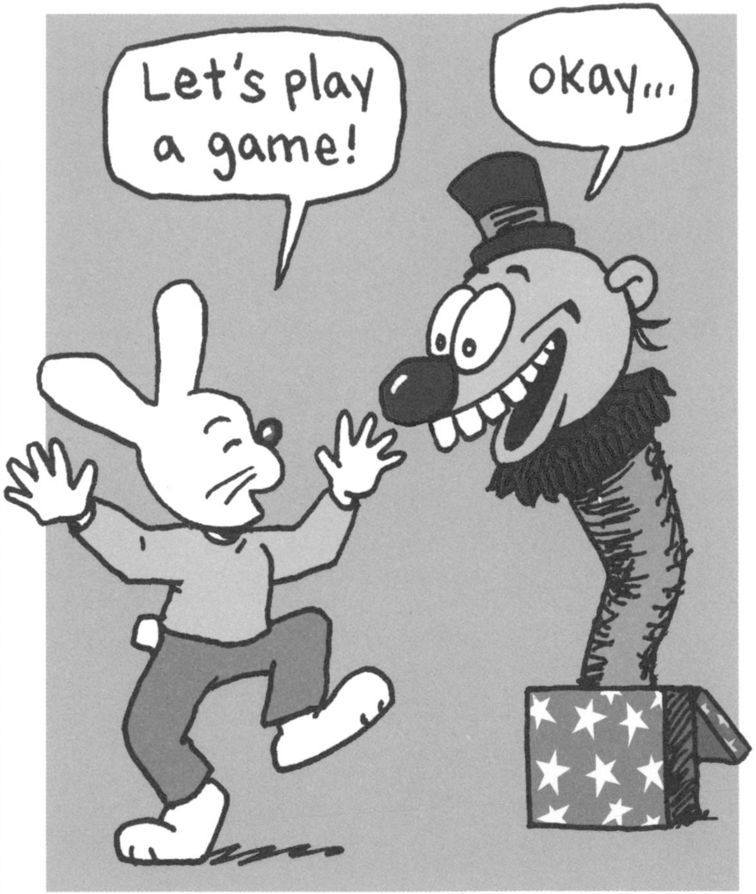
Let's play a game!
Okay...

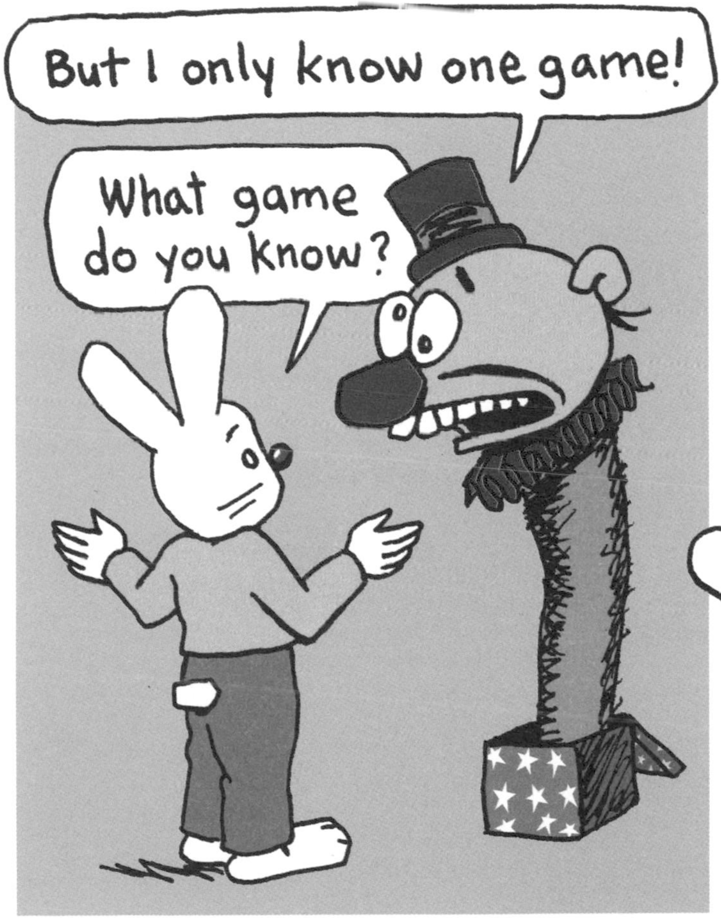
What game do you know?
But I only know one game!

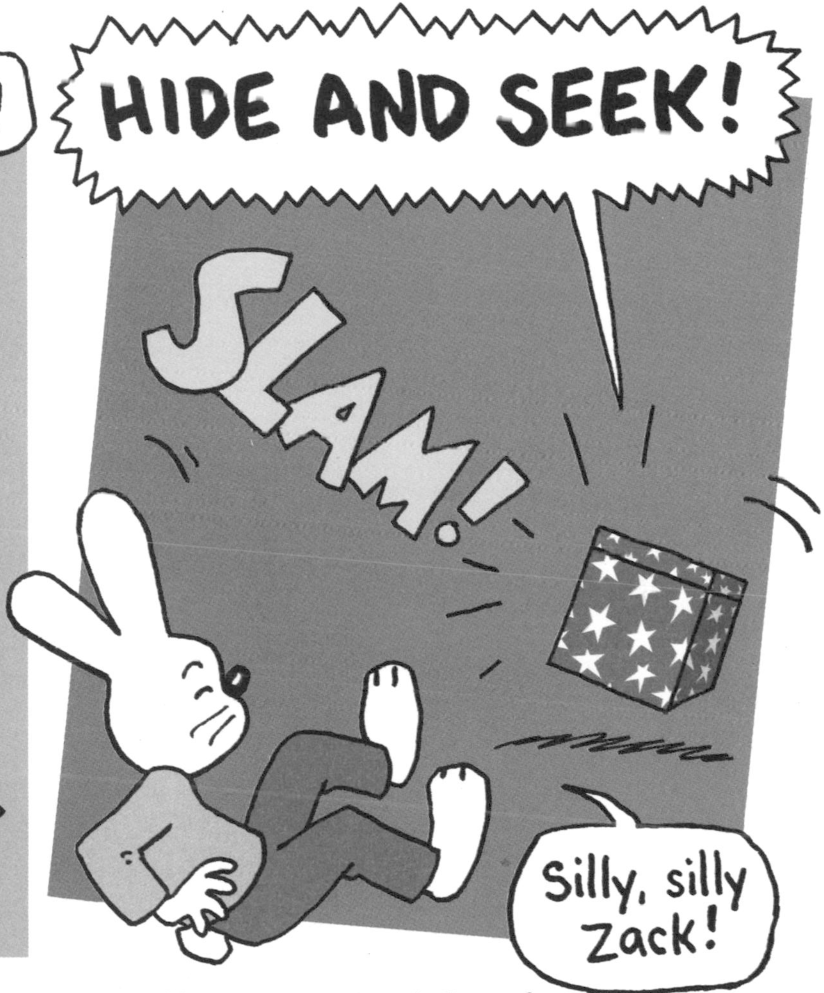
HIDE AND SEEK!
SLAM!
Silly, silly Zack!

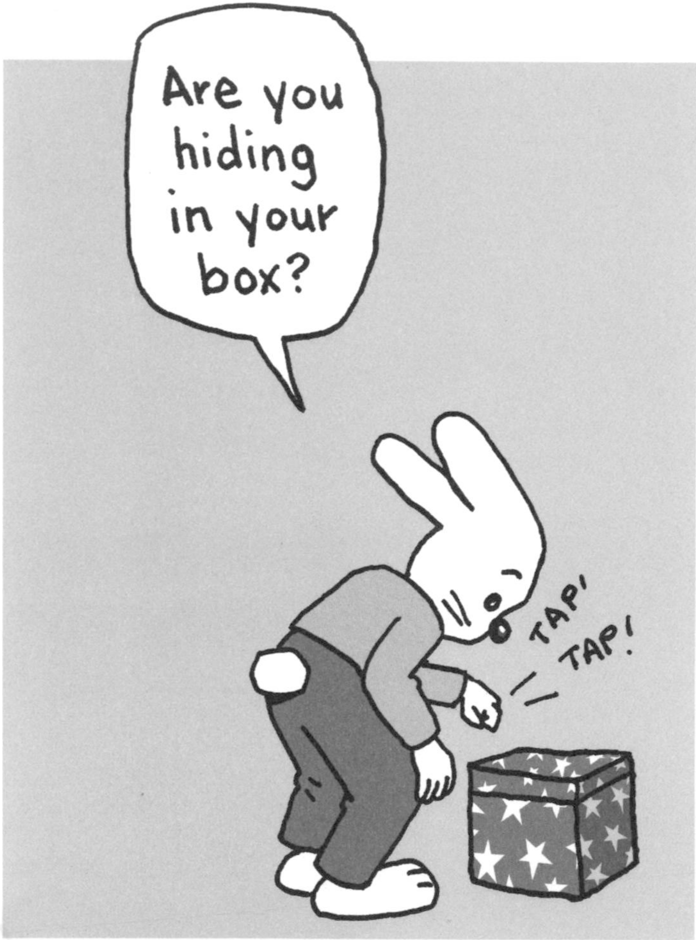
Are you hiding in your box?
TAP!
TAP!

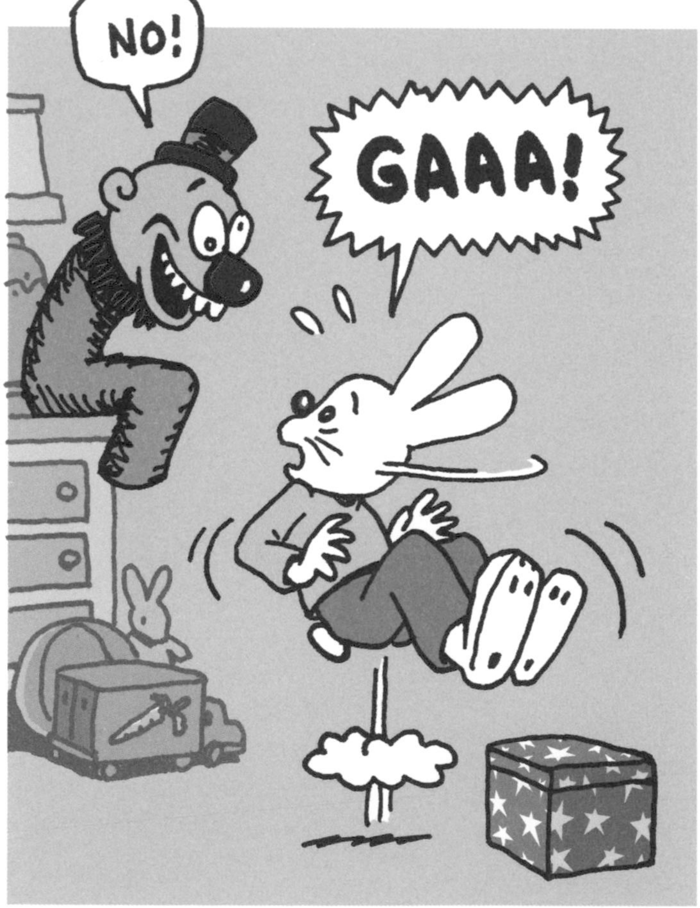
NO!
GAAA!

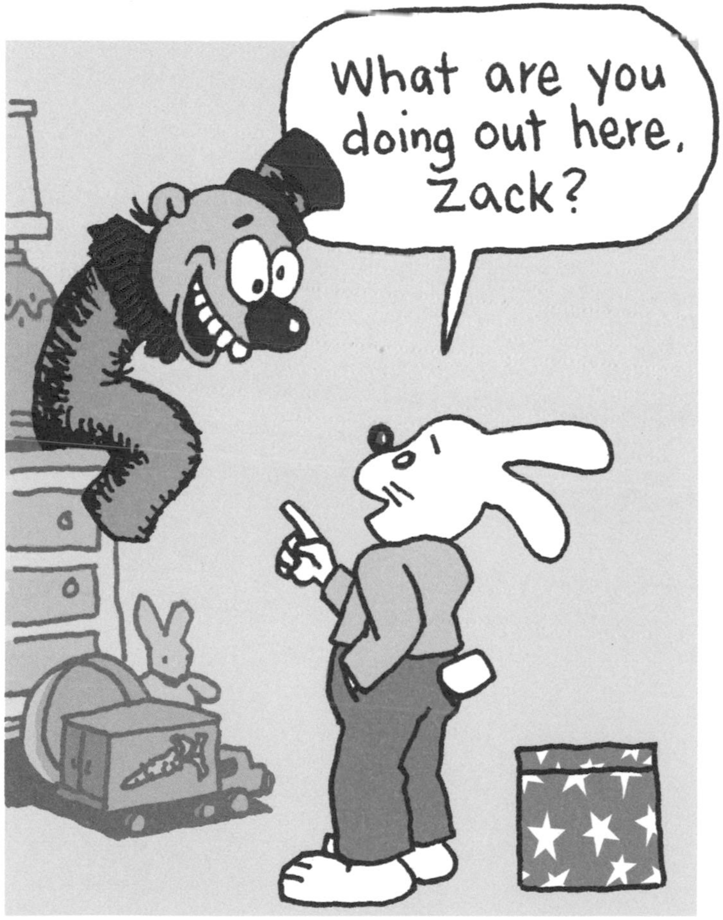
What are you doing out here, Zack?

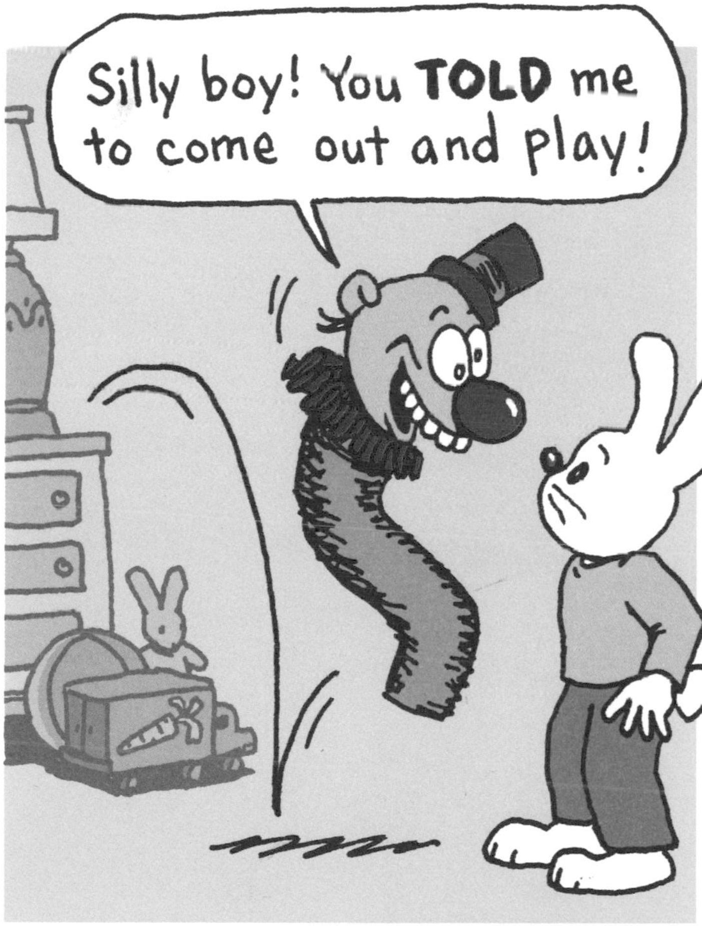
Silly boy! You TOLD me to come out and play!

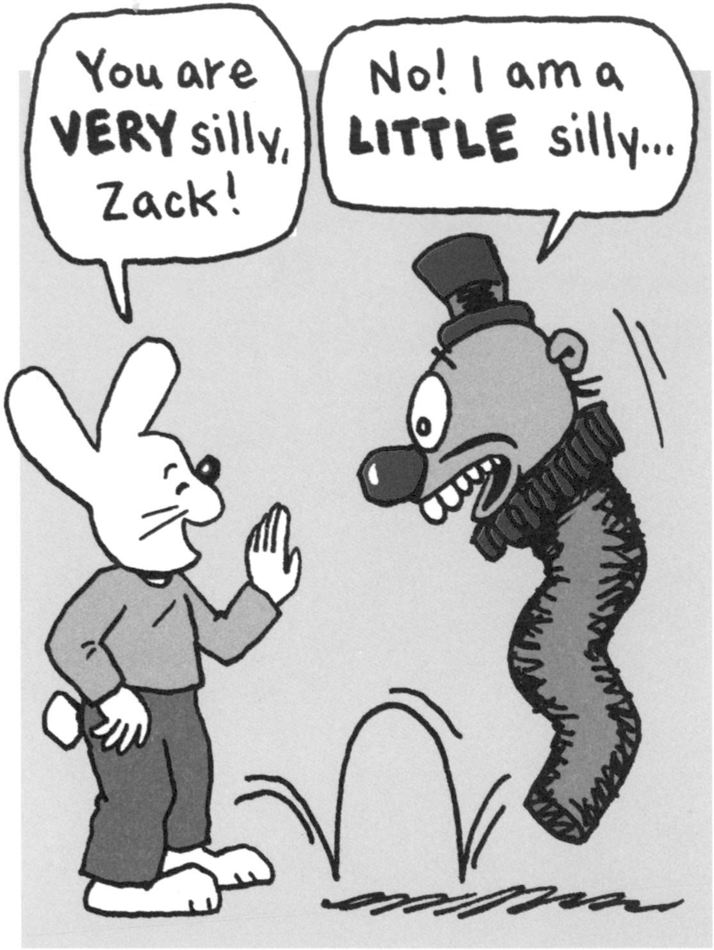
You are VERY silly, Zack!
No! I am a LITTLE silly...

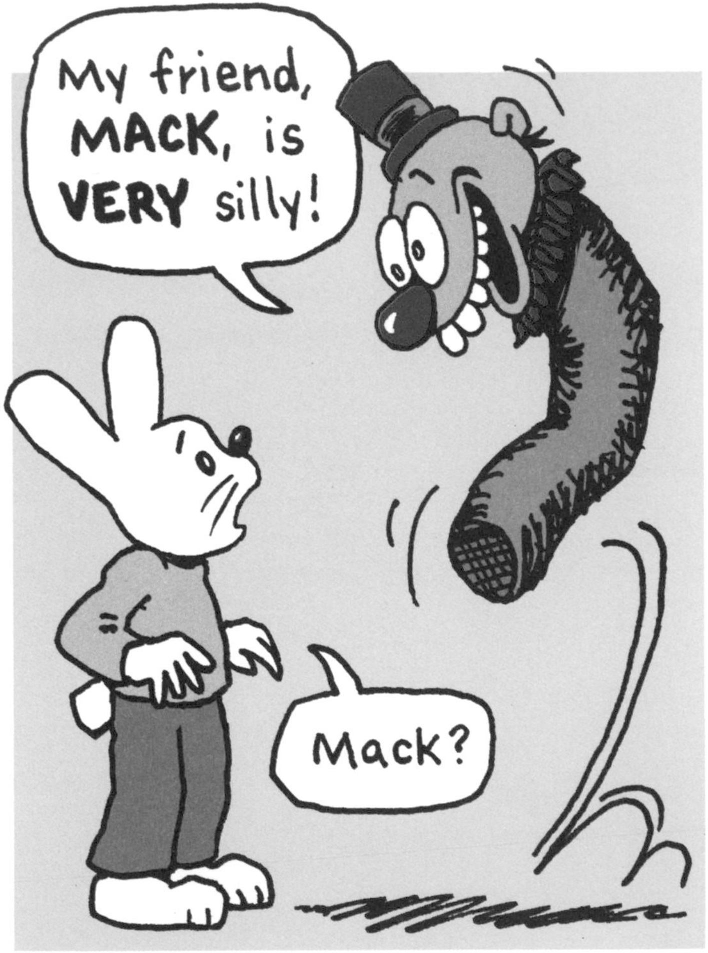
My friend, MACK, is VERY silly!
Mack?

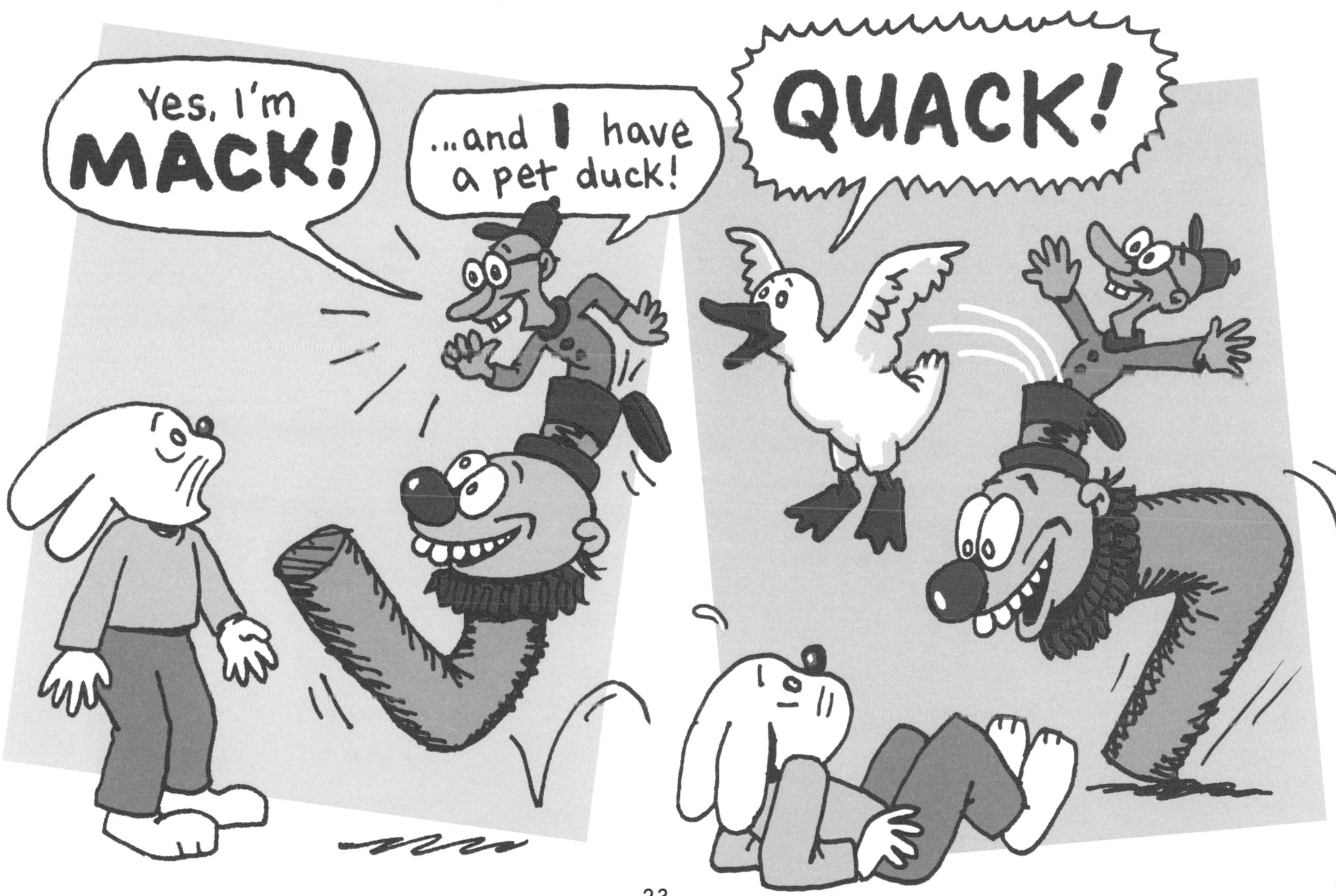
Yes, I'm MACK!
...and I have a pet duck!
QUACK!

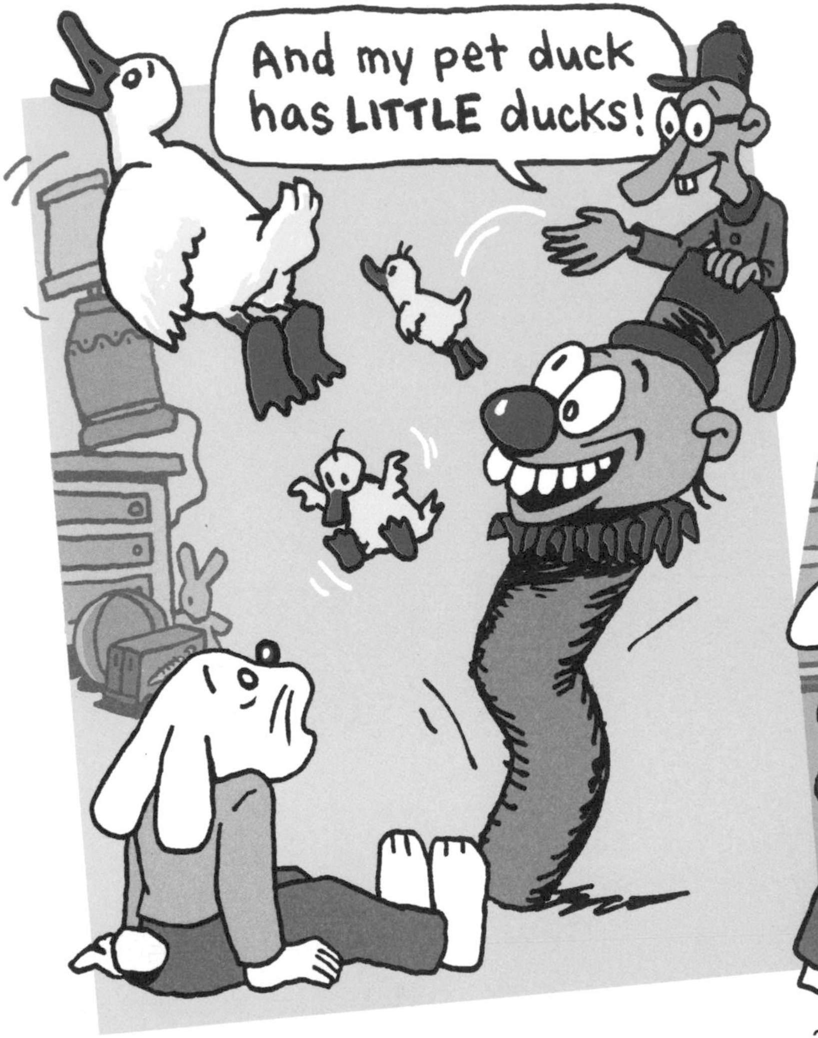
And my pet duck has LITTLE ducks!

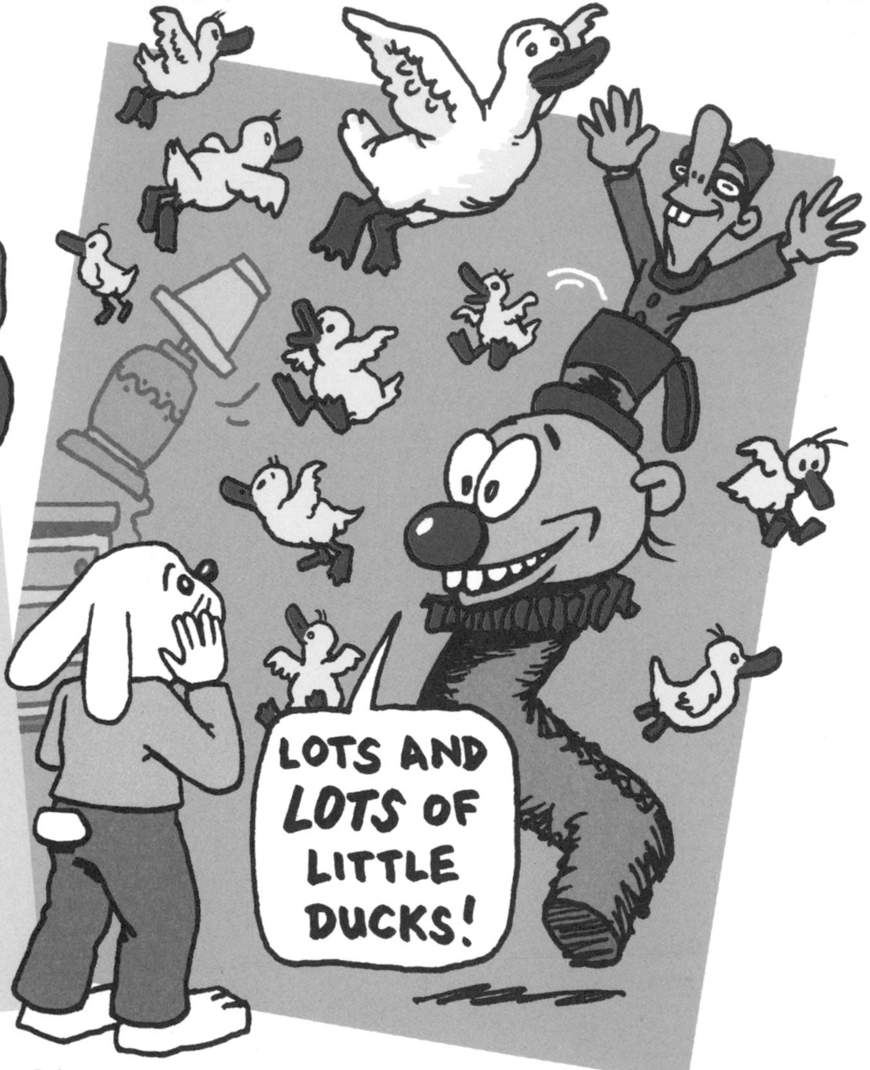
LOTS AND LOTS OF LITTLE DUCKS!

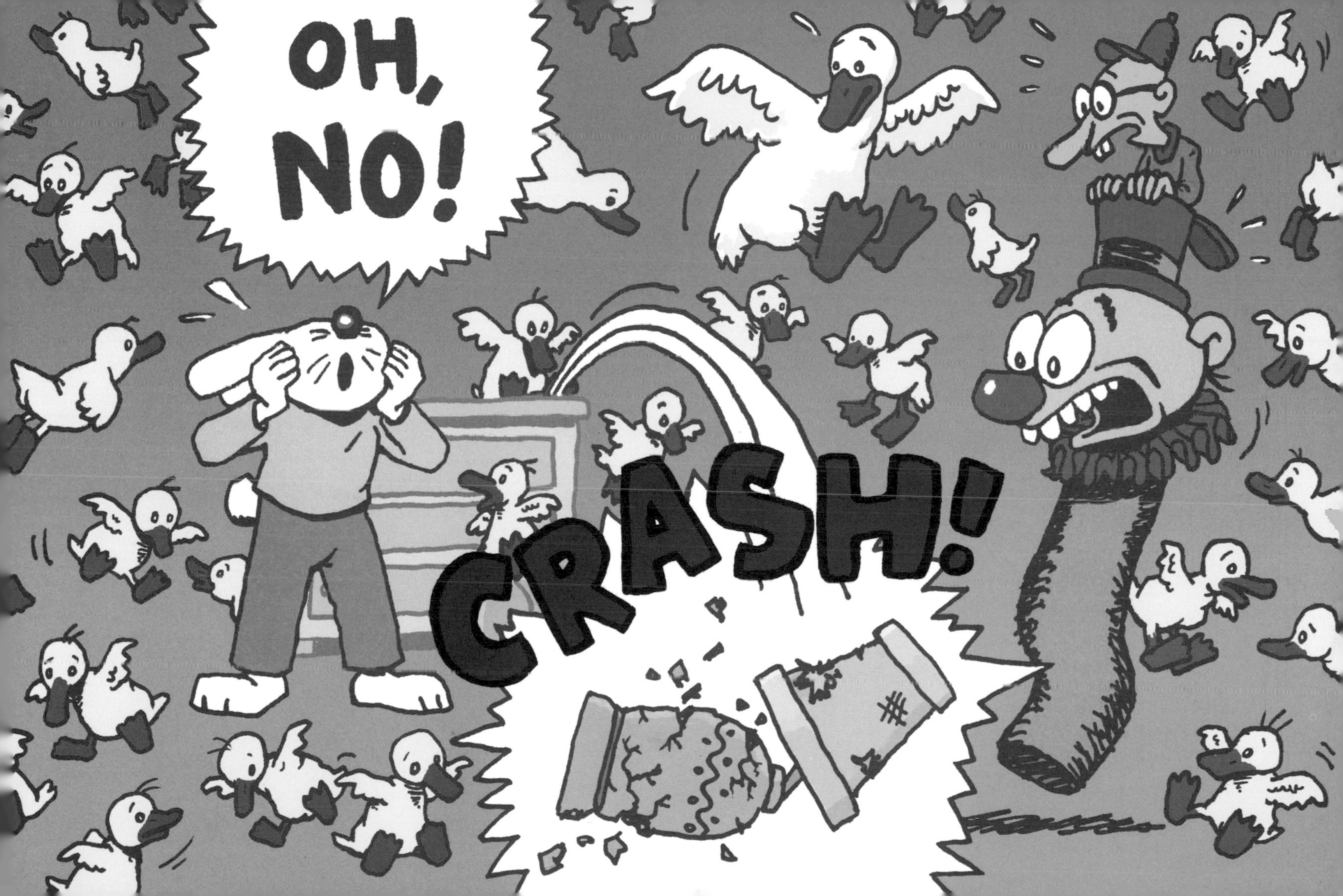
OH, NO!
CRASH!

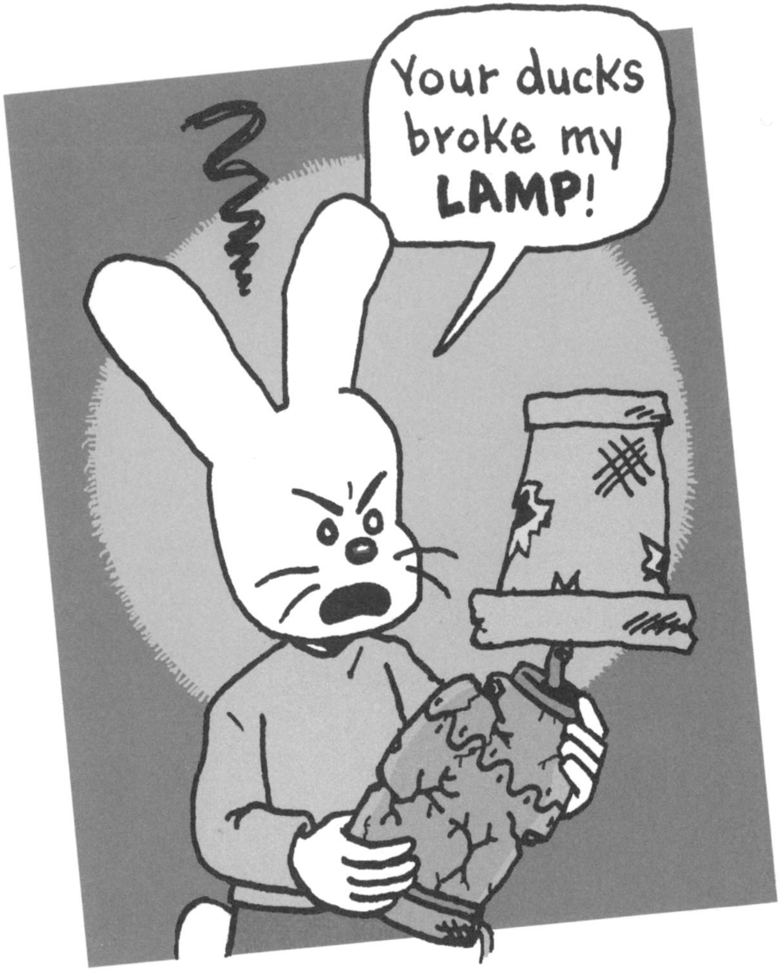
Your ducks broke my LAMP!

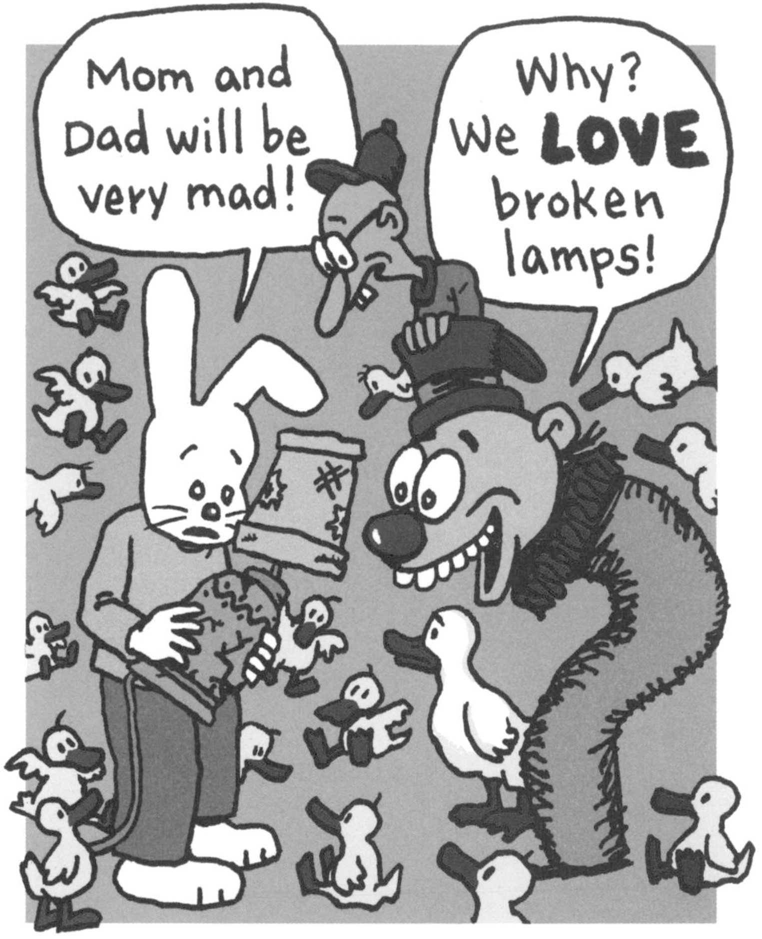
Mom and Dad will be very mad!
Why? We LOVE broken lamps!

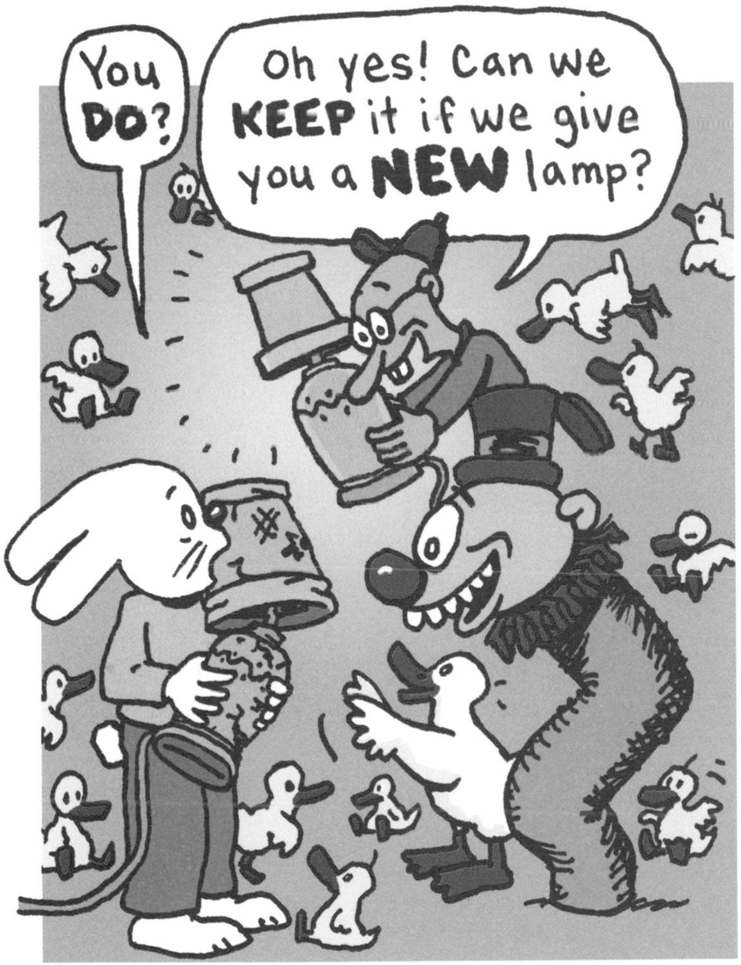
You DO?
Oh yes! Can we KEEP it if we give you a NEW lamp?

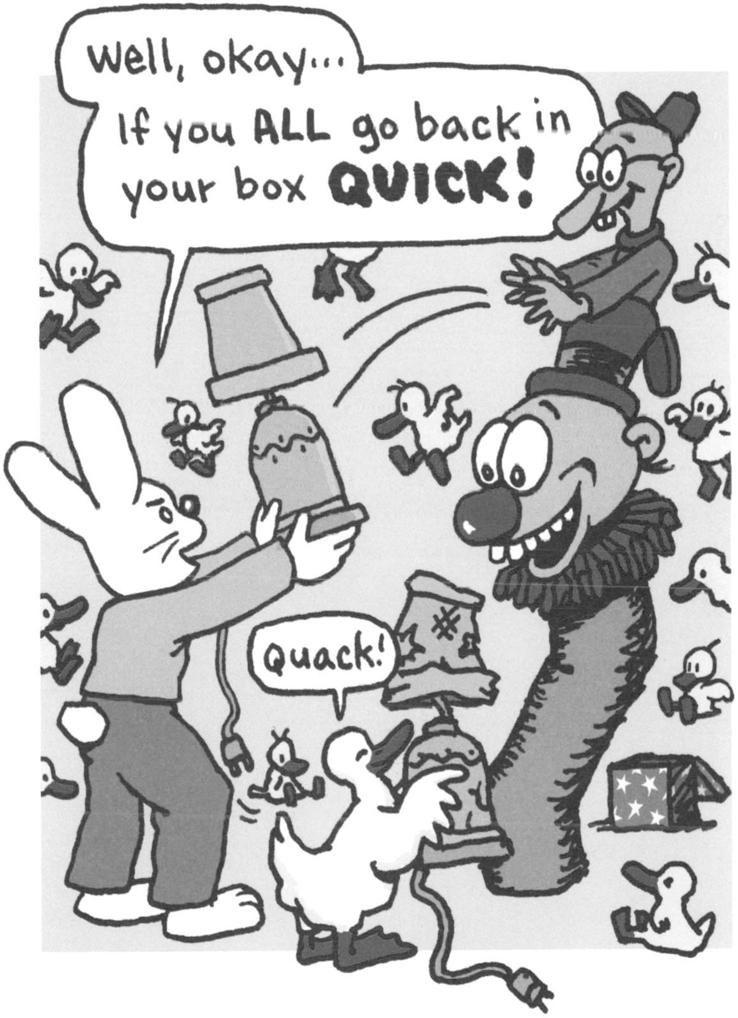
Well, okay... If you ALL go back in your box QUICK!
Quack!

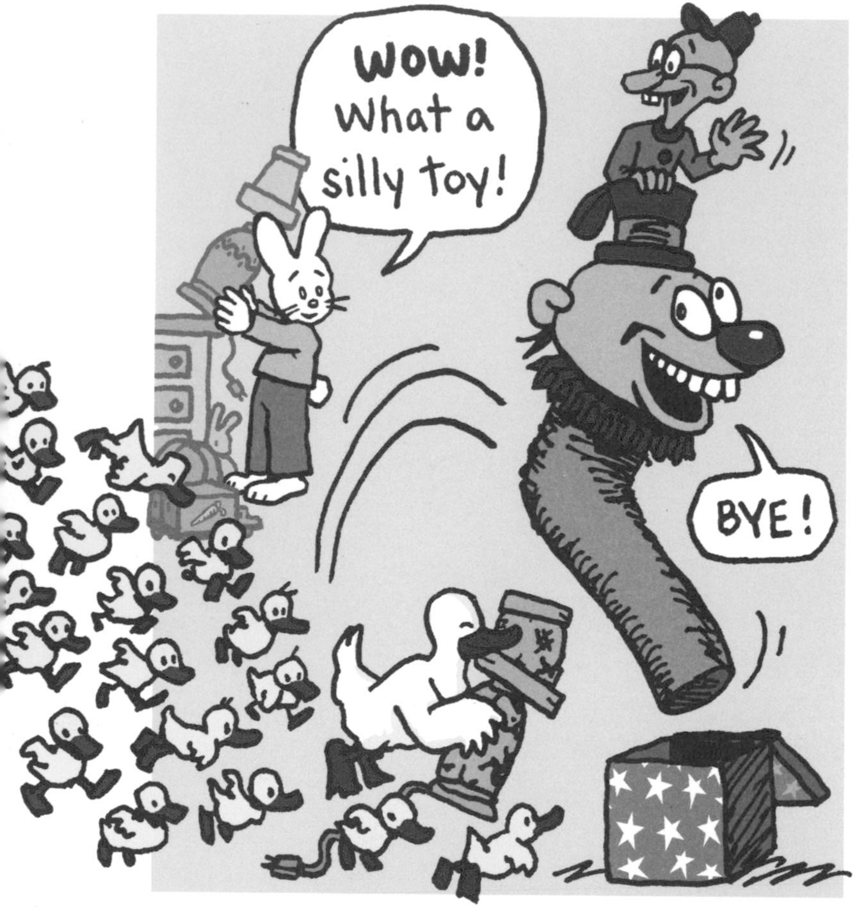
WOW! What a silly toy!
BYE!

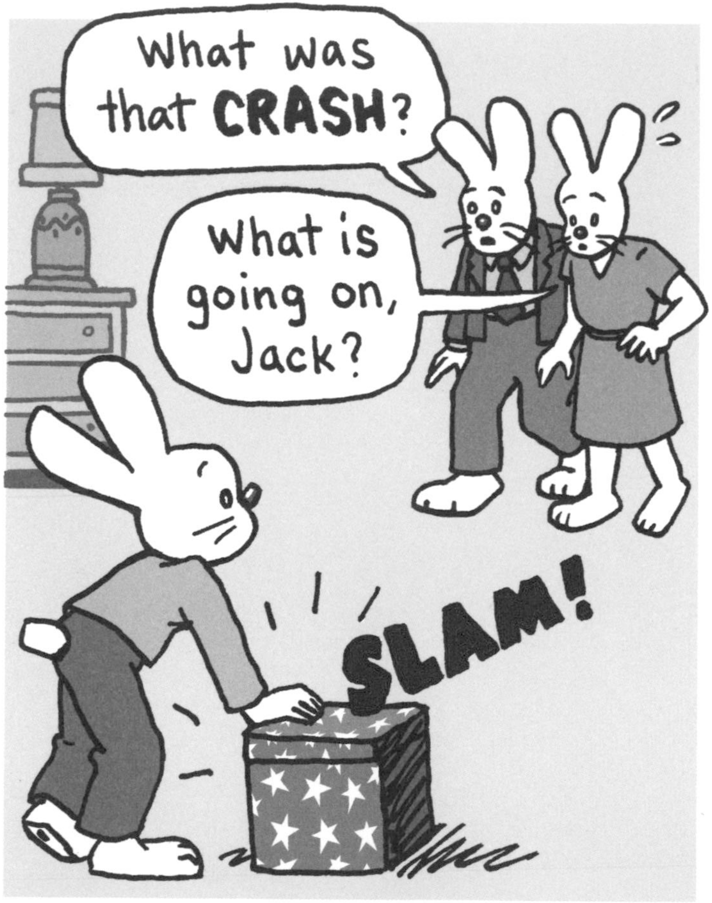
What was that CRASH?
What is going on, Jack?
SLAM!

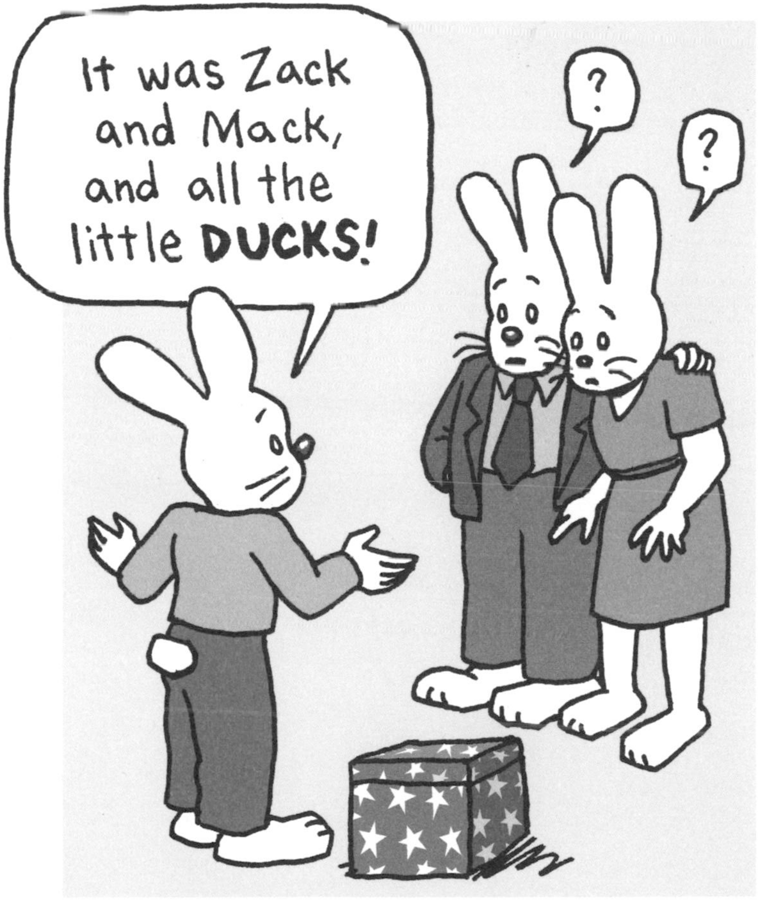
It was Zack and Mack, and all the little **DUCKS**!
?
?

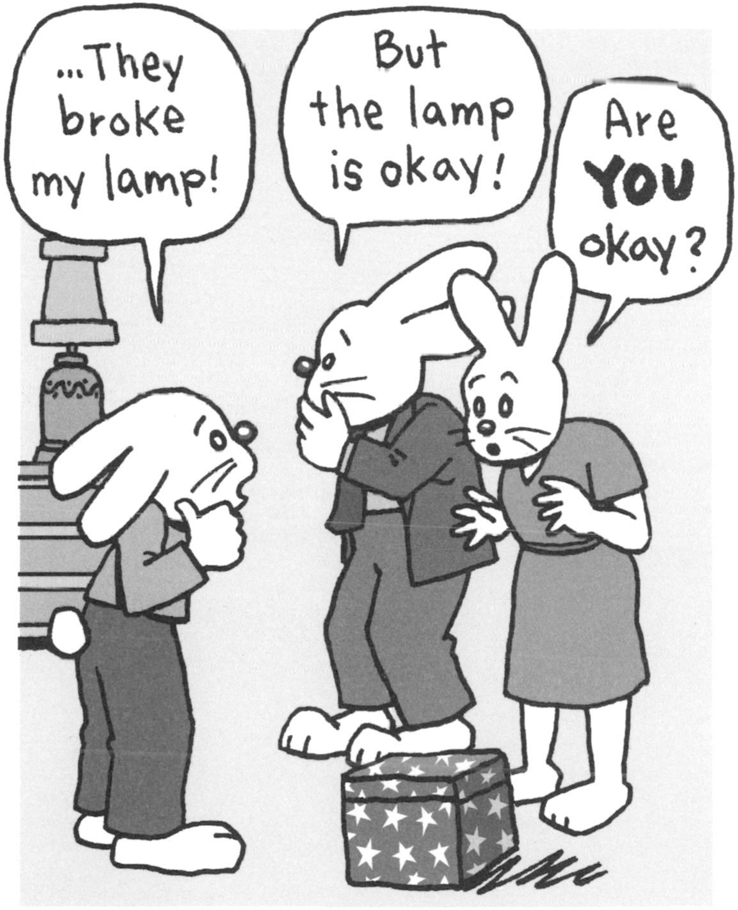
...They broke my lamp!
But the lamp is okay!
Are **YOU** okay?

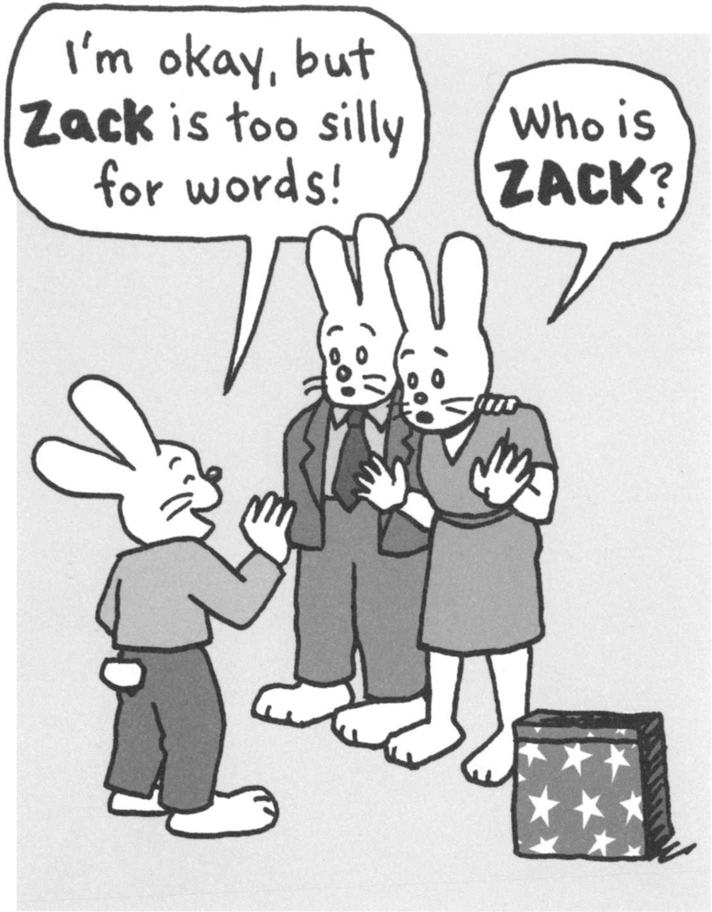
I'm okay, but ZACK is too silly for words!
Who is ZACK?

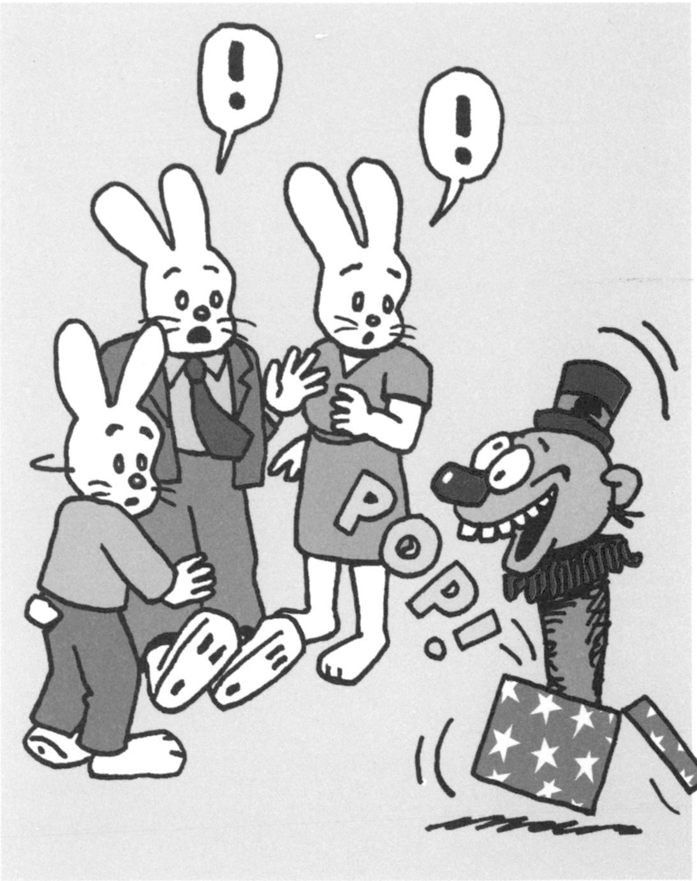
!
!
POP! POP!

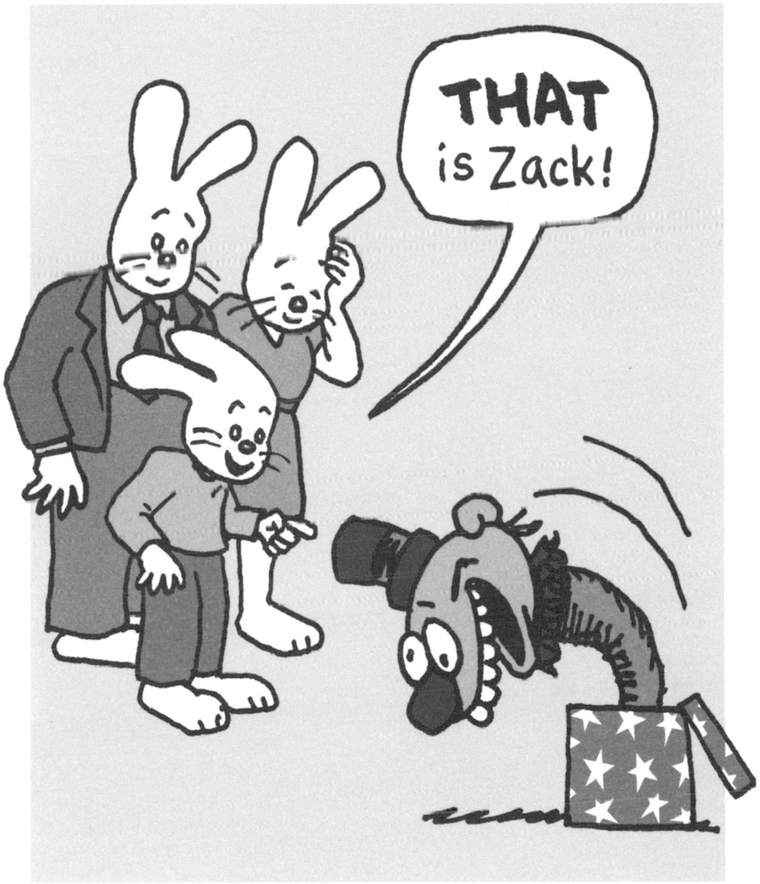
THAT
is Zack!

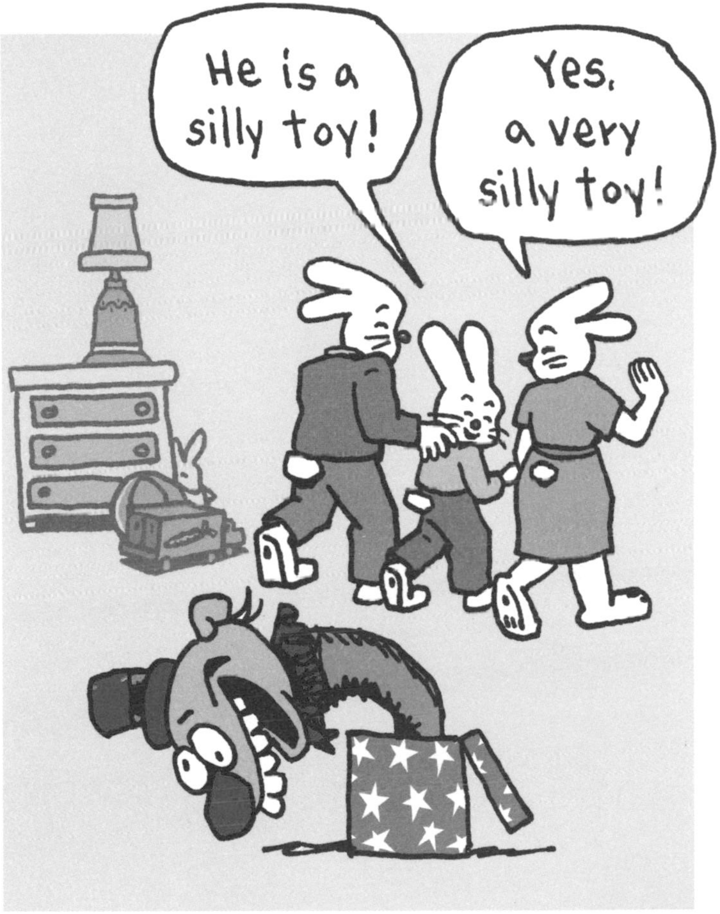
He is a
silly toy!
Yes.
a very
silly toy!

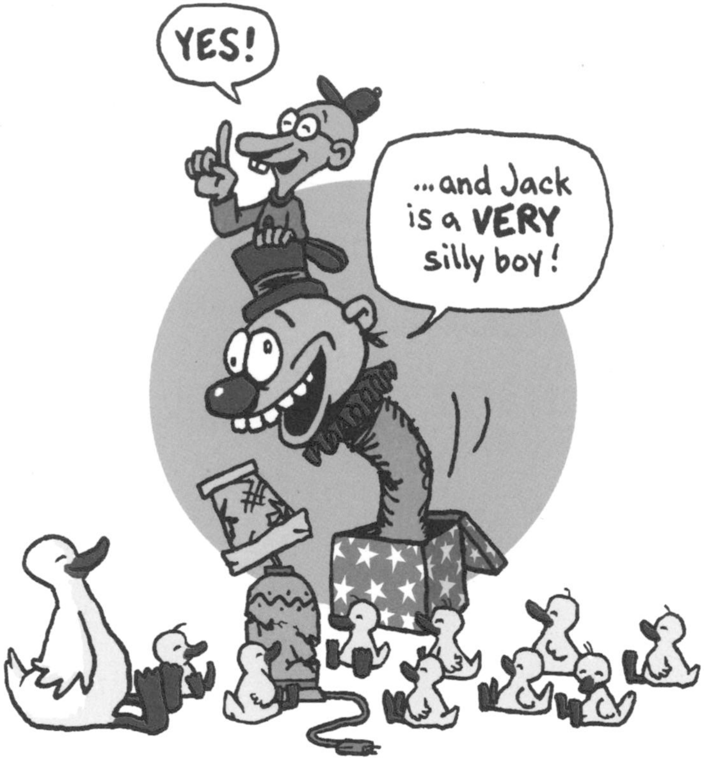
YES!
...and Jack is a **VERY** silly boy!

ABOUT THE AUTHOR

ART SPIEGELMAN learned to read from looking at comics, "trying to find out if Batman was a Good Guy or a Bad Guy." His now very grownup kids, Nadja and Dash, learned to read from comics, too. He says, "I sacrificed a very valuable collection of old comic books to fatherhood."

He is the author of the Pulitzer Prize winning *MAUS: A Survivor's Tale*. *BREAKDOWNS: Portrait of the Artist as a Young !@#%!* is his most recent book of comics for grownups. His work for children includes the best-selling *Open Me... I'm a Dog!* and the *Little Lit* series of comics anthologies, for which he was both co-editor and contributor. He and his wife, Françoise Mouly, live in New York City. Their cat, Houdini, never learned to read.

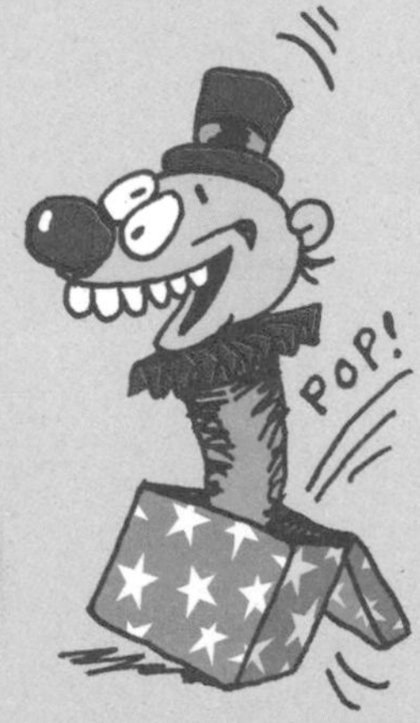
POP!